I0629501

Phantom Express

The Young Explorers, Volume 2

S T Cameron

Published by S T Cameron, 2025.

PHANTOM EXPRESS

First edition. July 11, 2025.

Copyright © 2025 S T Cameron.

ISBN: 979-8886230291

Written by S T Cameron.

To Chloe, Julian, Mae, and Jarrett

for whom I wrote these stories

Chapter 1

The engineer on the Dakota & Western Express leaned out the window of the steam engine and pulled the cord on the train's three-note Star Brass whistle to alert the stationmaster at Danford that the train would pull into the station in just a few minutes. He glanced over at the fireman, who checked the pressure gauge and then deposited a half shovelful of coal into the firebox.

The Dakota & Western Express, known simply as the Express to both its crew and the people of Danford, made the run from St. Paul to Spokane and back twice a month. Danford marked the end of the gently rolling prairies in the eastern part of the Dakota Territory. The tracks continued out of the station and sloped up to a bluff high over the Wakasica River, crossed a trestle bridge, and headed into the rougher lands in the western part of the Territory.

As the train approached Danford station, the engineer and the fireman were unaware that out on the trestle that crossed high above the waters of the Wakasica, a crude blockade made of logs and large stones had been constructed to prevent the train from continuing on its route.

The four men building the blockade were all well known around the Dakota Territory. The newspapers called them the Penny Ante Gang, named after two of its members, Jake Penny and Frank Ante.

Jake, the leader of the gang and a man with a very short fuse, hated that name and rumor said that he killed a man who repeated it to his face.

"That should do it," he said, wedging a log through the timbers supporting the track. "Let's go, Frank."

Frank dropped the stone he was carrying in a spot between two of the logs. "They can't get through this," he said and followed Jake off the bridge.

Frank Ante was a former locksmith who found that breaking open locks was a far more lucrative business than forging them. When his friend put a gang together, Frank was the first to join.

Two men waited for them at the end of the bridge.

"Grab the ax, Deacon," Jake told one of them.

"I'm Bishop. He's Deacon," the man replied, pointing to the other, who was his spitting image.

Deacon and Bishop Weston were the twin sons of devout Catholic parents who died in a prairie wildfire and were spared the shame that their sons had brought on their name. They were expert gunmen and wanted in several territories in connection with at least twelve murders.

"Whatever," Jake said. "Grab the ax and duck down over there. Drop the tree behind the train after it stops on the bridge."

"So it don't back up?" Bishop asked.

Jake rolled his eyes. He hated explaining the plan to the brothers. "That's right," Jake said. "So it doesn't back up." People thought the Weston brothers weren't bright and, unlike many of the rumors about their gang, that one was absolutely true.

"You and your brother will go through the cars and gather up all the valuables from the passengers," Frank said.

"What are you two gonna do?" Deacon asked.

"We'll be opening the strongbox in the baggage car," Jake said.

"The one with the gold?" Bishop asked.

"Not gold," Frank said, "cash. It's the payroll for all the forts in the Northwest."

"What about them guards?" Deacon asked.

"Frank and I will take care of them. You take care of the passengers," Jake said.

Deacon smiled at his brother. "Gladly," he said.

"How's the engineer going to know to stop?" Frank asked. "It's going to be dark, and they won't see the blockade in time."

"I told you, I've got that covered," Jake said. "Junior is getting on the train in Danford, and as the train nears the bridge, he'll tell them to stop. Don't you trust me?"

"I trust you, Jake," Frank said, "but I don't know this Junior. I don't trust anyone I don't know."

"You'll know him," Jake said. "Trust me."

Frank just nodded.

"Get into position," Jake said. "It'll be here soon."

On the Express, the last passengers in the dining car of the train finished up their dinners as the stewards removed the china, glassware, and silver from the other empty tables. One man took a last bite of his meal, a slow-roasted Andalusian-style lamb, and sent his compliments to the chef before heading back to the coach with his wife.

In the sleeper cars, the attendants made their way through the car, changing the seats into bunks. The sleeper cars were popular on long-distance trains, and many times, attendants overheard passengers say, "Thank God for the Pullman Palace Car Company."

While the sleeping accommodations were being made up, many of the passengers sat in the coach cars or the observation car, watching out the windows and trying to get their first glimpse of Danford.

The conductor pulled out his gold pocket watch and clicked it open. After quickly checking the time, he snapped it closed again and loudly announced, "Danford station, two minutes to Danford station."

On the platform in Danford, a small crowd had gathered. Most had been waiting inside the station. After the first whistle, everyone pushed out through the door and filled the small platform. The station attendants, preparing to load the luggage, tried to keep people away from the edge of the platform.

The crowd was equally divided between people who watched for the train to arrive so they could greet their returning loved ones, and people who gathered in small groups hugging and crying as they prepared to see their loved ones off on their journey.

The train whistle sounded again, much closer to the station. The energy of the crowd surged, and they pushed forward once again to the edge of the platform while the attendants tried to get them to stand back. Many were trying to be the first ones to spot the train as it rounded the bend and came into town.

The steam billowing out from the stack first appeared, much like a cloud above the roof of the Red Raven Saloon. Soon after, the engine came into view and the train slowed down as it approached the station.

Again, the whistle sounded. It scared a horse and sent it, and the wagon it was pulling, down the dusty street. The driver of the wagon yanked at the reins, trying to regain control.

Everyone was excited to see the train, everyone except for one teenager who stayed back in the shadow of the station doorway. He leaned out and glanced down the track at the approaching train and then ducked back into the shadows again. He pulled out his ticket and checked it again.

"First time on a train?" a woman asked him.

He jumped and turned toward the elderly woman, who smiled at him. Her blue eyes looked large through her round spectacles.

"Yes," the boy said. He glanced down at his bag, where the grip of the pistol Jake gave him was sticking out. "I mean no, I went to Chicago once." He kicked the bag behind him and hoped the woman hadn't seen it.

"Ah, now that's a city," the woman said. "Where are you headed now?"

The boy glanced at the ticket. "Butte," he told her.

"I'm going to Spokane," she said. "So, we'll be traveling part of the way together."

"Part of the way," the boy agreed.

The whistle and the noise of the engine as the train pulled into the station drowned out any further conversation. The people on the platform watched as the engine went by, followed by the baggage car and the dining car. The train slowed further and came to a stop with the coach cars alongside the platform.

Once the train had stopped, the engine let out a loud hiss of steam, and the engineer confirmed their arrival with one final blast of the whistle. The station attendants on the platform then went to work maneuvering the water crane to the engine so that the boiler could be refilled from the water tower that loomed over the station.

The conductor and three train attendants opened the doors of the cars and placed the steps in position. As soon as they were out of the way, the passengers destined for Danford disembarked. They flooded out onto an already overflowing platform and searched for any loved ones who were there to greet them. The hugs and handshakes began followed by some tears of happiness.

The huddled reunions, while joyful for the participants, blocked other people who were attempting to gather their baggage and leave the station platform. Once the platform in front of the cars cleared enough, the conductor looked at his pocket watch again. He nodded to the attendants and then they took their positions at the entrances to the cars to take tickets.

The boy looked at his ticket again. Although it wasn't a hot day, he was sweating. He wasn't sure why he let Jake talk him into it. He made it sound so easy. He said it would make him a man. Wasn't that what his father wanted?

"Grow up and be a man," his father told him when he cried. "Why can't you be more like your brother?"

He wasn't sure that he was a man like his brother, at least not a man who could rob trains. He looked down at the grip of the gun still sticking out of his bag. He had to decide what kind of man he wanted to be, and he had to decide soon.

The voice of the conductor cut through the noise of the people on the platform. "The Dakota & Western Express is now boarding for the territories of Montana, Idaho, and Washington with stops in Bismarck, Dickinson, Medora, Billings, Helena, Coeur d'Alene, and Spokane."

After one last goodbye to loved ones, the departing passengers pushed past the disembarked stragglers and lined up to get on board. The conductor and attendants checked their tickets, and they slowly made their way onto the train.

"Are you ready to board?" The old woman asked the boy. When she saw his hesitation, she added, "Maybe you can help a poor widow board the train." She tried to take his hand, but when she touched him, he jumped, and the ticket dropped from his hand.

The woman stepped on the ticket so that it didn't fly away in the breeze and carefully picked it up.

"Sorry I startled you," she said as she straightened up. "Here's your ticket safe and..." Her voice trailed off. The boy was gone.

She glanced around the platform, trying to find the boy, but there was no sign of him. When the conductor called, "Last boarding," the woman hurried toward the train and slipped the young man's ticket into her purse as she looked for her own.

Before long, the lines dwindled as the cars filled with the passengers from the platform. The conductor checked with the attendants to make sure everyone was on the train. He surveyed the platform and found that it was empty except for the baggage handlers.

He signaled to the attendants to close up the train and watched for any last-minute passengers.

The station attendants finished refilling the boiler and moved the water crane away from the engine and clear of the train. The conductor made sure all the cars were closed and picked up the step from in front of the last open door. He called out, "All aboard," and stepped up into the car.

The train whistle blew and after several puffs of steam rose out of the stack, the engine jerked forward with a groan. One after another, each car started with a sudden lurch. The conductor leaned out from the steps and watched as the train left the station. Once it was clear, he checked his pocket watch. He then closed the door and went about his business.

The passengers of the Dakota & Western Express settled in for the trip west as the train left Danford behind and began its climb to the top of the bluff and the trestle over the Wakasica River.

Jake took one last look at the tree they planned to drop behind the train. He listened to the tree groan as it bent in the wind. He had heard the train whistle signaling that the train had left the station. He hoped that the wind wouldn't cause the tree to fall too soon.

"Take cover, boys," he told the others.

Bishop, with ax in hand, ducked down behind the tree while the other three hid in some bushes farther down the tracks.

"He knows when to stop it?" Frank asked again.

"He knows," Jake told him. "Don't worry."

The fireman fed some of the coal into the fire to give the engineer the little extra power he needed to get the train up the incline to the trestle. It was slow going up the hill, but they both knew once they hit the top, the train would quickly reach its full speed.

The daylight was fading fast, so the engineer turned on the engine's headlamp. The headlamp had been kerosene until just the month before when they replaced it with an electric one. The engineer liked the new light. It was much brighter than the old one.

Jake and Frank watched the train from their blind as it came over the hill and headed toward the trestle.

"The engineer will slow soon," Jake said.

But the engineer didn't slow down. The train sped by them and headed out onto the bridge.

"It's not stopping," Frank yelled and ran out onto the track. "Can't they see the blockade?"

If anyone answered him, he couldn't hear it as the big tree fell across the tracks behind the train.

"There's the Lillian," the fireman said, pointing south along the river at a steamboat.

"That's the life," the engineer said, "just floating on down the river."

He looked out the window at the track ahead and saw the blockade in the train's headlamp. "What the..." he said and grabbed at the brake lever.

"Help me!" he yelled. The fireman grabbed the lever, and they both pulled with all their might, locking the wheels.

The brakes screeched as the two desperately tried to stop the train. As each car banged into the slowing car in front of it, the jolt threw the passengers and their belongings about the seats. The conductor, briefly thrown off balance, rushed ahead. He pulled his watch out and checked the time as if that would explain why the train was stopping so abruptly.

The engine could not slow enough before it hit the blockade. The branches in the barrier twisted and ripped the upper portion of the trestle apart. The engine rode up on top of the barrier before it slid sideways and fell off the side of the bridge.

The rails split and bent as the supports below the center portion of the bridge broke apart and collapsed into the river below it.

The passenger cars remained connected to the engine and followed it over the edge of the bridge. The conductor was trying to move between the cars when they fell, and he stumbled. He dropped his watch as he tried to regain his balance, but fell out when the cars tipped over and dropped to the river below.

The engine hit the water and immediately sank to the bottom. The wooden luggage, dining and coach cars hit one after another and broke apart, scattering baggage and bodies across the water before the next car crashed down on top of it.

The Pullman cars were next, followed by the observation car at the end. As the last car came down, the boiler of the engine exploded, throwing super-heated water and debris into the air and blasting apart one of the bridge supports, causing more of the bridge to collapse down onto the broken cars.

Then everything was silent.

In the days after the accident, newspapers from Chicago to San Francisco, and even as far away as New York, carried stories about the great Dakota & Western train wreck in the Dakota Territory. Within a week, they captured all the members of the Penny Ante Gang except for Jake, who the posse killed in a shootout.

The three remaining members were tried for the deaths of the more than one hundred passengers and crew of the Express in a sensational trial that was reported in the newspapers for more than a month.

In September 1883, the court convicted the three outlaws on all charges and hanged them five days later.

Right until their execution, they claimed that there was another member of the gang known as Junior, but the authorities never found him.

Chapter 2

A dark red Packard led the caravan of vehicles across the prairie of North Dakota. Although the land was relatively flat, the dirt roads were extremely bumpy and uneven. Combined with temperatures that had to be close to the century mark, that made eleven-year-old C.J. Kask uncomfortable as he sat on the bench seat next to his father, Angus.

Angus Kask was the leader of an archaeological expedition headed to Danford on the Wakasica River in central North Dakota. His team was commissioned by the Chicago Museum of Archeology to look for additional artifacts from the Dakota & Western Express train wreck that crashed into the Wakasica River over 30 years earlier.

Following the Packard was a black Ford Model T belonging to Walter MacGregor, an archaeologist on the team, and his wife, Edna, the team's botanist. Their two children, Sadie and Scotty, were sleeping in the back of the car. Mr. MacGregor chose black for the Model T because, as Henry Ford said, the car can be "any color the customer wants, as long as it's black."

Behind the Model T, Jackson Hall drove his blue Jeffrey. He and his wife, Teresa, were the anthropologists on the team. Their daughter, Laura, sat in the back, trying to read a book about hieroglyphics. Her mother could never figure out how she could read in the car with the book bouncing around in her hands.

The last vehicle in the caravan was a Clydesville truck driven by Roland Everett, the Chief of Operations for the expedition. Axel van Housen and his son, Frederick, were also riding in the truck's cab. Axel was in charge of security and was an expert in weapons and ammunition. His son was only thirteen, but he was quickly becoming an expert on arms as well.

It had been a long drive, and everyone was glad to arrive in Danford in the early afternoon. The town was home to over 3000 people, yet the streets and yards were almost deserted. Most of the residents were staying indoors out of the hot summer sun.

They easily found the main street of the town, which was, of course, called Main, and followed it down to the railroad tracks. C.J. pointed out the Empire movie theater. The marquee advertised Cleopatra, starring Theda Bara.

"Did you want to see it?" his father asked him.

"Nah," C.J. said. "I'm waiting for The Adventurer."

"The Adventurer? That sounds like one you'd like. Who stars in it?"

"Charlie Chaplin."

They passed a gas station, and that reminded Angus that they would need to fill before heading out to the site. A sign in front of the station said that gas was 21 cents a gallon. "Gas is expensive out here," he told his son.

The train station was at the end of Main Street, and the caravan slowed down as they turned onto Elm Street in front of it. There was a banner across the street side of the train station declaring that the election for mayor of Danford was a week away. Other signs were for the candidates, with another large sign announcing a debate the next evening right there in front of the station.

Although there was no train at the station, several people waited on the platform. C.J. could see a line of older boys, probably in their late teens, standing with their duffel bags beside them. An older man in uniform was apparently marking their names off a list he was holding.

C.J. looked at his father.

"They're probably headed off to boot camp," Angus told him. "After that, they're off to Europe."

C.J. nodded. He heard that there was fighting going on in Europe. 'The War to End Wars', they called it. He didn't know what the fighting was about, but he hoped it would end all wars.

The caravan continued on to a large warehouse next to the train station. A sign painted on the front of the building showed that it was the Danford Historical Museum. They parked the vehicles in front of the building and stepped out to stretch after their long drive.

When they entered the museum, the first thing they saw was a large, damaged smoke stack from a steam train mounted on a block of black marble. On the slanted front of the marble block was a plaque listing dozens of names. It was a memorial to the people who died in the great Dakota & Western train wreck of 1883.

"Is that the actual smoke stack from the train that crashed?" C.J. asked.

"Sure was," a voice piped up from behind them.

They turned to find a rather short rail of a man in a light brown suit sporting a thin handle-bar mustache and round glasses. He was smiling at them.

"The name is Eugene Emerson," he said.

"Are you the curator?" Angus asked, stepping forward to shake the man's hand.

"Yes, I am," he told them. "Would you be Mr. Kask, by any chance?"

"I would," Angus said. "And these are members of my team." Angus introduced everyone.

"Welcome gentlemen," Emerson said. "And ladies," he added quickly, pulling on his forelock. "I am so glad you are here. Anything you can do to add to our little collection would be welcome."

Emerson showed them through the doors into the main room of the museum. The large room was full of displays, most of which concerned the Dakota & Western Express.

A man with a bow tie who appeared to be in his fifties was looking into a display case in the center of the room beneath a skylight. The case displayed a diorama of a broken trestle with train cars hanging off of it. He glanced up at them and then went back to examining the scene.

"Is the museum only about the train?" Edna asked.

"Oh no, dear lady," Emerson said. "It is about the proud history of the city of Danford." He glanced around the room at the different displays. "Well, the train wreck is our biggest draw, but it's not all. Why, right over there, we have busts of all the mayors of Danford since it became a town." He pointed toward the far corner where two busts stood side by side.

"Don't pay any attention to them," a man said from the entrance to the room. He was a tall man with dark hair and a white Stetson. His cowboy boots clomped across the floor as he approached the group.

"Speak of the devil," Emerson said. He introduced the man to the others. "This is Jefferson Danford. He is the mayor of our town."

"Danford? Are you related to the founder of Danford?" Angus asked.

"I sure am. He was my father and the first mayor of Danford," Jefferson said.

"Jefferson Danford, Sr.," Emerson said. "This one is Jr."

"I dropped that," Danford told Emerson sternly. He turned to the others. "No need to make a distinction, since my father passed on years ago."

C.J. noticed the man who had been looking at the diorama and was standing at a display closer to them.

"Were you in Danford when the train crashed?" Teresa asked Emerson.

"Oh, no," he said. "I'm not from here. I moved here to run the museum. Besides, I would have been two."

"I guess you wouldn't have remembered it even if you had been living here," Teresa said.

"No, but Mayor Danford was around," Emerson said. "You were a teenager, weren't you?"

"I was pretty young then," he said. "But I wasn't in town. I was off at boarding school."

The man with the bow tie began a coughing fit.

"Are you all right, Henry?" Emerson asked him.

"I'm fine," Henry said when he recovered. He continued to examine the display and ignored the group.

"Oh, this is Henry Penn," Emerson said. "He's a long-time resident of Danford and running against Mayor Danford in the election next week." Emerson thought for a moment. "Say, Henry, you were here when the train crashed, weren't you?"

The man shook hands with everyone except Mayor Danford. "Welcome to Danford," he told them. "And yes, I was in the area when the train crashed. I grew up on my parents' farm a few miles north of here."

"Maybe we can talk about that time," Angus said.

"I'm not sure that I can be of any help to you," Henry said. "I was pretty young."

Emerson looked at his watch. "I supposed you want to get settled in and get an early start."

"We hoped to," Angus told him.

"Do you have any other questions that I can answer for you?" Emerson asked.

"Just one," Angus said, looking at a note he pulled from his pocket. "Where can we find the Prairie Rose Boarding House?"

The Prairie Rose was a grand Victorian home that had been built by Elmore Wesley, one of the original settlers of the area, when his Angus cattle ranch made him a rich man. A few winters after building the stately mansion, the man died in a terrible blizzard that not only took his life, it also wiped out most of his herd.

The tragedy left his widow, Mrs. Ruth Wesley, with too many debts, and she had to sell off the land until all she had left was the house. She turned the mansion into a boarding house and took in renters in order to feed herself and her two young children. Angus arranged with her granddaughter, now full-grown and living in Portland, to stay in the house for the three weeks they planned for the dig.

They parked in front of the house and unloaded their bags. A black wrought-iron fence surrounded the house, and the front yard was not in the best of shape. The grass needed mowing, and the flowerbeds were over-grown with weeds. The house itself, once a grand building, had peeling paint and several shutters were hanging askew.

They entered the house using the key that the granddaughter had left with the curator the last time she was in town. The inside smelled of dust and a hint of mildew. Angus found a light switch and pushed the ON button. Everyone was relieved when the lights came on.

The furnishings were plush, and the heavy drapes over the windows added to the darkness of the house. A thin layer of dust seemed to cover everything. C.J. wondered how long it had been since anyone had lived in the house.

They all took their bags upstairs and spread out to find rooms. While the adults found rooms on the second floor, C.J. and the other kids climbed the stairs to the third floor. Sadie and Laura found a nice girl's room with two beds. Frederick staked his claim on a large bedroom. C.J. and Scotty found a dreary but acceptable bedroom that they could share.

C.J. opened the drapes to let the sun into their room. From the window of their third-floor room, C.J. saw the tops of both trestle bridges spanning the river. His father told him that rather than rebuilding the old trestle and disturbing the place where so many people died, they built a new trestle a short way upstream from the old one.

"Come down once you're settled in," Edna called up the stairs. "We'll have ourselves a late lunch."

The MacGregors teamed up to create a delicious meal of picnic sandwiches and fruit that they purchased from the corner grocery. They served it in the large and ornate dining room of the house. At first, they opened the drapes, but the sun was too bright, so they closed them again.

They served the meal on some fine blue china with flatware that Teresa Hall said might be real silver. They sat down around the table and ate.

The conversation immediately turned to the train, the trial of the Penny Ante Gang, and the hanging.

"Please, I'm eating," Mrs. MacGregor said. "Let's not be talking about the crash and people hanging. It gives me the creeps."

"It gives me the creeps too," an elderly woman said from the dining room doorway. Everybody jumped.

After a moment, Roland stood up. "Sorry, Ma'am. You startled us," Roland told her. "Can we help you?"

The woman placed her eyeglasses on a sideboard and smoothed out her blue flowery skirt. "I'm sorry I startled you. I just wanted to introduce myself to my guests. I'm Ruth Wesley."

"Ruth Wesley?" Angus asked. "Your granddaughter didn't mention that you still lived here."

"Oh yes, this house looks run down," she told them, "but it isn't empty. I've been here since my husband and I came out here from Indiana."

"We assumed the house was empty," Edna MacGregor said. "I'm sorry, we made ourselves at home."

"That's fine," Mrs. Wesley said. "I want you to make yourselves at home. I'm glad to have someone stay here again. My granddaughter doesn't come to visit much, and it gets lonely out here all by myself."

Mrs. MacGregor went around the table, introducing everybody to Mrs. Wesley, who happily greeted each one. When the introductions were done, Angus stood up and pulled out a chair for the old woman, who sat down and smiled at everyone.

"You were here when the train crashed into the river?" C.J. asked.

"C.J.," Angus admonished him.

"No, it's perfectly all right," Mrs. Wesley assured Angus. She turned to C.J. "Yes, young man, I was here in the summer of 1883. It was a warm August, like this one."

"What do you remember about that time?" Mrs. MacGregor asked.

"It was a terrible thing. So many people died," she said, shaking her head.

"Did you know any of the people?" C.J. asked.

"Oh yes," she said. "Many of the people were going from here to there and simply passing through Danford. I knew some others very well."

She clasped her hands in her lap and looked down at them. "It was a sad day. Many people in town rushed out to the river to see if they could help, but the passengers were beyond all help." She looked up at all the faces around the table. They all listened intently to her. "Afterward, I came home and just cried. I don't think I left the house for days."

Jackson Hall gave her a glass of water. She smiled and drank a sip. Then she continued. "A sadness lay over the town and lasted until well after the funeral."

"There was only one?" C.J. asked.

"Only one, yes," Mrs. Wesley told him. "We had one funeral for all twelve people from Danford who died in the crash. I was there and saw the sadness and loss in all their faces."

She took another sip of water.

"After the funeral," she continued, "they had the trial and then they hanged those poor boys."

"Poor boys?" Teresa Hall exclaimed. "They caused the deaths of everyone on the train."

"Yes, they did," Mrs. Wesley said sadly. "They were bad boys. Still, I don't believe in hanging."

Everyone was quiet for several minutes, and then Mrs. Wesley spoke again.

"They all went back to their lives thinking that was the end of that," she said. After a pause, she added quietly, "but it wasn't."

"What do you mean?" Angus asked.

"Ever since that night, we've heard it coming through town every few days, headed for the old trestle," the old woman said.

"Hear what?" Mrs. MacGregor asked.

"Isn't that what I've been trying to tell you," Mrs. Wesley said, "It was the ghost train." She glanced out the dark windows. "It was the Phantom Express."

Chapter 3

They were up before the sun the next day and prepared for a long day out in the heat of a North Dakota summer. The MacGregors reprised their roles as chefs to make a light breakfast of oatmeal with leftover fruit from the night before and some homemade biscuits.

While most of the team pitched in to pack lunches for the day, Angus went to let Mrs. Wesley know they wouldn't be back until after dark. He knocked on the door to her room, which they were relieved to find out wasn't a bedroom that they had commandeered. There was no answer.

He tried the door and, finding it unlocked, opened it a crack to see if she was still sleeping. In the growing light of the morning, he could see that Mrs. Wesley was not there, and she made the bed for the day.

When he returned to the main floor, he noticed some flowery luggage in the entry to the house. After some more searching, he found Mrs. Wesley sitting in the dim light of the front parlor, working on a cross-stitch project.

"Good morning," he said. "I wanted to let you know we will be out all day and won't be back until after dark."

"That's fine," Mrs. Wesley said without looking up from her handiwork.

"It's not my business," Angus said, "but I noticed you packed some bags. Are you going on a trip?"

"Oh, I will be out for a while today," she said. "I should be home late tonight." She held up the linen to check her work. "I'll try not to disturb you when I come in."

"That won't be a problem," Angus said. "I hope you enjoy your outing."

They packed up what they needed for the day and headed down toward the river. They crossed the railroad tracks on the way out of town. While the train tracks headed up the slope toward the twin trestle bridges that spanned the river valley, the road they followed wound around the hills and down toward the river itself. The bridge used by cars and wagons was much lower than the railroad bridges that towered over it.

Before the road reached the bridge, there was a turnoff that allowed vehicles to access a little park along the river, which was perfect for picnicking and a day of swimming. The park was also the best way to access the area below the old trestle where they would look for artifacts from the train wreck.

When they parked their vehicles near the beach, they found a curious thing. Because of the drought in the area, the river was no longer anywhere near the beach. In fact, the river, which was normally almost a half-mile wide in many places, was only a small stream four feet across, looping around through the center of the mostly dry riverbed.

The beach was a sandy hill that dropped off sharply toward the bottom of the riverbed. Getting their equipment to the site and back was going to be difficult.

As curious and interesting as that sight might have been, it was literally overshadowed by the two massive trestle bridges that towered over the beach on either side.

The old trestle downstream from them still stood close to two hundred feet high and had a large section of the middle missing. They built the new trestle, which was upstream, in a similar fashion. Both bridges had towers a quarter of the way up and a trestle construction above it. The towers allowed boats and debris to pass under the bridge.

"That's where the boiler blew out one tower," Angus said, pointing to the two shattered pylons that jutted up from the dry riverbed.

"The cars landed around the engine in that same area," Jackson said. "That's where we will work."

"How did they get the engine out?" C.J. asked.

"They brought a barge up from farther south in the Territory," Angus told him. "The explosion blew almost everything apart. It was just a pile of splintered wood and ripped metal."

As they silently thought about the devastation, a train crossing on the newer bridge blew its whistle.

They hauled their gear down the slope and out onto the dry riverbed. C.J. noticed the bones of dead fish embedded in the packed surface of the riverbed. They had gotten stuck in small pools as the water receded.

"We have to watch for bad weather," Edna warned everyone. "A good rainstorm here or even someplace upstream can send a flash flood down on us."

"Like in Johnstown, Pennsylvania?" Scotty asked.

"Yes, and no," Edna said. "In Johnstown, a dam broke and caused that flood. I was thinking more of Heppner in Oregon about fifteen years ago."

"What happened there?" Sadie asked.

"It had been a dry spring, and heavy rains caused a wall of water fifty feet high to go through the town," she said. "Over two hundred people died."

More than one kid glanced up river at the sky when they heard that.

"We'll keep an eye out," Sadie said.

Once the equipment had been hauled out, they set up a tent as a base of operations where they could get out of the sun and protect their equipment from the wind and any possible rain. Inside, they laid out a diagram of the site that the curator provided them and mapped out where they wanted to start their search.

While Jackson marked off a section of the riverbed with stakes and string, the others brought tools they would need to sift through the hard packed silt.

C.J. noticed a rotting board sticking a few inches out of the ground nearby. He could see a bit of green paint on the splintered board.

"Is that from the train?" he asked his father.

Angus glanced over at it. "Maybe," he said. "Hard to tell. We'll check it out when we search that area."

The adults carefully dug into the riverbed with their hand tools, depositing the earth into sifters they used to find any small items hidden in it. They gave the five kids their own tools to help, and at first, they were excited to see what they would find.

The sun crept up over the eastern ridge of the river valley and baked the riverbed. After more than an hour and a lot of digging and sifting, they had found nothing. The kids took frequent breaks in the tent and soon didn't return to the digging.

Instead, they spent their time wandering around looking for anything they could find that was sticking out of the ground. Except for the one board, they found nothing that way either.

At one point, Teresa Hall cried out that she'd found something. They all gathered around and watched as she carefully removed the object from the silt. She placed it on a sifter and used a brush to remove some of the sand that adhered to it.

"What is it?" C.J. asked excitedly.

Teresa carefully lifted it and turned it over. "It appears to be a lady's purse."

"Is it from the train?" Sadie asked.

Teresa brushed it a little more. "It's hard to tell. We'll have to wait and see, I guess."

"Is there anything inside?" Frederick asked.

"It's too fragile to open just yet," she told them. She took it into the tent to work with it more while the others went back to work with renewed energy.

Before long, the kids, bored again, looked for something else to do.

"Is there anything more exciting we can do?" C.J. asked his father.

Angus smiled at him. "It's slow, tedious work, I know. Not everything is fast and exciting."

The kids looked disappointed.

He looked at them thoughtfully. "Maybe I have something," he said and disappeared into the tent.

When he returned, he had a brown box. "I brought a Brownie in case we wanted to take pictures."

"Can we use it?" C.J. asked, reaching for the box.

"Hold on," Angus told him. "Let me show you how." He showed them how to hold it against their stomach and look down through the viewfinder on top to line up the picture.

He then pointed out the exposure lever on the side and told them to hold their breath as they pull down on the lever so that breathing won't cause the camera to move and blur the picture.

Finally, he taught them how to wind the film to the next position so that they didn't take several pictures on the same film.

"You can only take six pictures with each pack of film, so find six interesting objects to photograph," he told them and handed them the camera.

Sadie took the first picture. She told the adults to hold still and snapped a picture of them digging in the riverbed. She wound the film until the number two appeared in the exposure window, and handed the camera to Laura.

Laura aimed the camera at the old trestle bridge and snapped a picture. Then she wound the film and handed it to Frederick.

Frederick led them out to the edge of the stream running through the middle of the riverbed and took a picture of a section of the bridge that was torn apart. They all heard the bridge creaking loudly in the wind that blew through the river valley.

"Is it going to fall?" Laura asked, monitoring the old bridge.

"Someday," Scotty said, "but probably not today. They design bridges to withstand the wind. They'll sway and creak, but they won't fall down. This bridge has been standing for over thirty years."

Frederick handed the camera to Scotty.

"I want to take a picture farther up," Scotty said, pointing up the long slope toward the top of the bridge.

The others agreed. They let the adults know where they were going and they headed out.

Angus glanced up the slope. "Be careful," he said. "And stay off the bridge."

"We will," C.J. called back.

They returned to the beach and followed the access road back toward the main road. There, they discovered a rough path that others had used to climb from the beach up to the top of the bridge.

"What do you think happened to the money?" Frederick asked the others.

"What money?" Scotty asked.

"The money that the train robbers were after," Frederick said, "the whole reason the train crashed."

"They didn't intentionally crash it," Sadie told him. "They wanted to stop it."

"I know," Frederick said. "Some guy named Junior was supposed to stop the train."

"Do you think there was a Junior?" Scotty asked.

"I think so," Sadie said. "If there wasn't, their plan wouldn't make much sense."

"Do you think he's still in Danford?" Scotty asked.

"I would've left town right away," Frederick said.

"That would be too suspicious," C.J. said. "I think he stayed. Who knows, he might still be in town."

They were almost at the top when Scotty stopped. "There," he pointed, "that's a good picture." He took a picture, looking out along the side of the bridge.

He handed the camera to C.J. as they continued up.

When they reached the top, they found a long dead tree lying across the tracks where the train robbers had dropped it. The train tracks, unused for almost thirty years, were reddish brown with rust.

They followed the tracks to the edge of the bridge and looked out across it. It creaked in the wind.

"They look like ants," Scotty said, pointing down at their parents far below. Everyone leaned out to look down.

Everyone, except Frederick.

"What's wrong?" Sadie asked when she noticed he was hanging back.

"I don't like heights," he told them. He glared at the others. "And if anyone says anything, I'll—"

"What's that?" Laura said, pointing at the bridge.

Light reflected off of something below the tracks partway out on the bridge. Everyone squinted to make out what it was.

"It looks like something gold," Frederick said.

"Do you think it's valuable?" Scotty asked.

"Part of the gold shipment," Frederick said.

"I don't think there was gold on the train," Sadie told him. "I think they said it was cash."

"We should get it," Laura said, quietly, the reflected light flashing across her face.

"I wouldn't go out there," C.J. said. "Besides, my dad said to stay off the bridge."

C.J. took a picture out across the bridge and wound the film to the last exposure. "Let's go back down and tell them what we found."

They all turned and headed back to the path. Laura remained, staring out at the light flashing off the object.

"Come on, Laura," C.J. called. She didn't move.

Sadie took her arm. Laura pulled away.

"I found it," Laura snapped at her. "It's mine."

"What are you talking about?" Sadie asked.

C.J. called to them again. "Come on, you two."

Sadie turned to C.J. "She won't go," she told him.

When she looked back, she saw Laura was out on the bridge, making her way out to where it hung.

The others rushed to the edge of the bridge. They wanted to call out to Laura and get her to come back, but they didn't want to attract the attention of their parents far below. They saw her stumble in the wind.

"She's going to be blown off the bridge," Sadie said in a panic. "How are we going to get her back?"

C.J. glanced down at the riverbed below and the people down there that were unaware that one of their kids was in danger of falling off the bridge. Without thinking, and before anyone could protest, C.J. was out on the bridge trying to catch up with her.

C.J. didn't hear Sadie when she called to him. He was too far out on the bridge, and the wind was strong and loud. It buffeted him as he kept his head down and concentrated on not falling between the crossties. He tried not to look beyond the rails to the riverbed.

Ahead of him, Laura stopped above the object hanging from a beam ten feet below the tracks. She stood there for a moment and tilted her head as if she were curious about something.

Before C.J. could reach her, she kneeled down, grabbed the rail, and climbed over the side.

"Laura," C.J. yelled. "Get back up here."

Laura didn't appear to hear him. She worked her way down until she was standing on the beam where it was hanging. From where C.J. was staring down at her, he could see that it was a gold pocket watch hanging from a chain that was caught on a nail sticking out of the beam.

Laura crawled out along the beam until she reached the pocket watch. She unhooked the chain from the beam and looked at it.

"Get back up here. Now!" C.J. called to her.

She placed the watch in her pocket and backed up along the beam until she was below C.J.

She started to climb up to the roadbed. C.J. lay on the tracks and reached down to give her a hand. As she reached up, the support broke loose, and C.J. watched his friend fall backward off the bridge.

Chapter 4

It was almost as if everything had happened in slow motion. The supports that Laura hung on to broke. The expression on Laura's face changed from the impassive one that she'd had ever since she'd seen the pocket watch hanging from the beam to a surprised, horrified one as she fell backward, still clutching the broken pieces of wood in her hands.

C.J. reached out to grab her arm, but she was too far away. He could do nothing except watch her fall toward the riverbed far below.

Then, one broken support landed with one end on the beam where the watch had been and the other one on the end of another beam next to it. Laura's fall came to an abrupt stop, and miraculously, she kept her grip on the board. The other support pulled from her other hand and fell like an arrow toward the ground. Seconds later, it skewered the river bed with a loud thwack.

The vibrating board got the attention of the adults on the ground. They saw C.J. leaning over the edge of the bridge and Laura hanging from the supports. The yelling and running began instantly.

C.J. knew that she could only hang on for a short time. Then, either her strength would give out or the board, which was dangerously bent, would break. He had to move fast. He climbed over the edge and made his way down the same way Laura had earlier.

He inched out onto the beam until he was at one end of the support that Laura was clinging to. He laid flat along the beam and reached down to Laura's free hand. She grabbed it and briefly hung suspended, stretched between his hand and the wood support.

She let go of the support and grabbed at C.J.'s arm as she swung below the beam where C.J. lay. He held on to the beam with his legs and his other hand while Laura climbed up on top of him and slid back under the tracks until she was sitting on the beam.

C.J. sat up and carefully turned around on the beam until they were facing each other.

"Are you all right?" C.J. asked. A shout from above interrupted Laura's answer.

"Are you two OK?" Angus called down.

C.J. nodded but didn't take his eyes off of Laura.

"We're sending down a rope. Tie it around both of you and we'll haul you up," Roland called as he dropped the end of a coil of rope over the edge.

C.J. slid up closer to Laura and tied the rope around both of them using a bowline knot. They then wrapped their arms around each other as the two men hauled them up to the tracks. Once there, they climbed up over the edge and back onto the top of the bridge.

Once the adults untied them, Angus and Roland walked them back along the tracks and off the bridge. The rest of the group waited for them on the bluff.

Teresa Hall hugged her daughter tightly and then began checking her for injuries. "Are you all right?" she asked. "Does anything hurt?"

Laura said nothing and stared at her hands.

"What were you doing?" Teresa asked the girl.

"I think we should get them back home," Angus interrupted. "We can talk about that later." He gave C.J. a look that told him there would be a serious talk after Laura was safely back at the house. C.J. looked away and avoided his stare.

They helped the kids down the path back to the beach. While the rest went back to work, Angus and Teresa loaded C.J. and Laura into the Packard and drove them back to the house. After they'd pulled up in front of the house, Teresa helped Laura to her room, and Angus sat down with C.J. in the front parlor.

"What happened up there?" Angus asked.

C.J. told his father the whole story of how Laura had walked out on the bridge and fell.

Later, Angus and C.J. tapped on the door to Laura's room, and Teresa let them in.

Laura was asleep in the bed covered completely with the heavy, blue and green flowery comforter that matched the decor in the room. Her rhythmic breathing confirmed to C.J. and his father that she was sleeping.

"She fell asleep right away," Teresa told them.

"How is she?" Angus asked.

"Her arms are sore, which is not a surprise after hanging from the side of a bridge."

"Did she say what happened?"

"She said nothing," Teresa said. "She was distant, as if she were someplace else."

Angus looked at C.J. and nodded to him.

"We went to the top to take the last two pictures," C.J. began. "Laura saw something on the bridge."

"What?" Teresa asked.

"It was a gold watch," he said. "We didn't know what it was at first. We all agreed to tell you about it and let you figure out how to get it."

"That was wise," Angus told him.

"At least I thought we had," C.J. continued. "Next thing we knew, Laura was out on the bridge."

"Why didn't you call for help?" Teresa asked.

"I don't know," C.J. said. "I wasn't thinking. I saw the wind almost blow her off the tracks, and I just ran out." He paused and looked over at Laura.

"What happened then?" Angus prompted him.

"She climbed down before I could get there," C.J. told them. "She got the watch, and when she was climbing back up, she fell."

"What happened to the watch?" Angus asked.

"She'd put it in her pocket before she tried climbing back up," C.J. said.

Teresa went to Laura's dress, laid out on the other bed, and checked the pockets. She turned back, dangling a gold pocket watch by its chain from her hand. She handed it to Angus.

Angus looked at the watch carefully, turning it over in his hands. There was an etching of flowers and leaves across one half of each side and a braid around the edge. "It certainly is clean and bright. It couldn't have been hanging there for long," he said.

"Are there any markings?" Teresa asked, looking over his shoulder.

"Not on the outside," Angus said and clicked the watch open.

On one side was the watch face with the words, "F. L. Nasham" and "Nevada, IA" written in a script font. The watch stopped at 1:13.

In the watch cover facing it was a picture of a stiffly posed woman wearing a fancy hat. Angus carefully hooked his fingernail under the edge of the picture and pulled it out.

Angus read the inscription beneath the picture.

To my beloved Cal,

May the rails always lead back home.

Love, Maggie

"Could it be from the train?" C.J. asked.

"The picture certainly looks appropriate for the time," Teresa said, examining it.

"And the reference to the rails connects it with trains," Angus said. "Still, it isn't positive proof."

"It could be," C.J. insisted.

"It is possible." Angus told him. "I'll have to talk to Emerson about it. He might have some information at the museum about this Cal and Maggie."

"What if he does?" C.J. asked.

"Then he'll add it to the museum's collection."

"Add what?" Laura asked. She tried to sit up in bed, and when she saw that Angus and C.J. were in the room, she pulled the covers up to her neck. "Add what to the museum's collection?" she repeated.

"How are you, sweetie?" Teresa asked.

"My arms and neck are sore," she said. They could see her stretch one of her arms under the covers. "What happened? How did I get here?"

"Don't you remember?" Teresa asked. She looked over at Angus, who was also concerned.

"All I remember is climbing to the top of the bridge to take a picture," she said.

"You remember nothing about when you were at the top of the bridge?" Angus asked.

"No," she said, "nothing. The next thing was just now when I woke up."

"Did you have any dreams?" C.J. asked. Both Teresa and Angus looked at him curiously.

"Well, I remember something about gold light," she said, closing her eyes and trying to remember. "There was gold light shining in my eyes and then I stumbled or fell."

"You don't remember walking out on the bridge?" her mother asked.

"No," she said, alarmed. "I wouldn't go out there. It was creaking, and I thought it was going to fall."

"We'd better wait until later to talk about this anymore," Angus suggested, getting to his feet and heading to the door. "We should let Laura rest."

"Can I have my watch?" Laura asked. Everyone stopped where they were.

"What watch, sweetie?" her mother asked.

"Mine. The gold one," she said.

"This one?" Angus asked, holding the watch so she could see it.

Laura smiled. "Yes," Laura said.

"Where did you find it?" Teresa asked.

"I didn't find it," Laura said. "I've always had it."

He went to the bed and handed it to the girl.

She pulled her arms out from under the comforter and took the watch. She clicked it open and gazed at the picture of the woman on the inside. She gave a slight smile. "She's pretty. Isn't she?"

"Yes, she is," Teresa said.

Laura clicked the watch shut and held it by the chain to look at it. As it twisted on its chain, the light from the lamp reflected off the watch into her eyes. A distant look came over her face, and her hands, still holding the watch, fell limply into her lap.

"Sweetie?" Teresa said.

Laura continued to stare without seeing. She didn't respond to her mother.

"Sweetie?" Teresa repeated. "Are you all right?"

When she still didn't respond, Teresa tried to take the watch from Laura.

Laura was suddenly back and clutched at the watch. "No, it's mine," she snapped.

Teresa pulled away from the girl.

Laura continued, as if nothing had happened. "Oh, it stopped," she said and wound the watch.

When she was done, C.J. spoke softly to her. "That watch is valuable to you, isn't it?"

Laura looked at C.J. She looked a little confused. "Yes," she said after a moment, "yes it is."

"You want nothing to happen to it, do you?"

Laura's eyes widened, and she clutched the watch to her tighter. "No, I don't."

"We can put it someplace safe while you rest."

"Someplace safe?" Laura asked.

"My dad has a box downstairs with a lock," C.J. said. "If we put it in there, nothing will happen to it."

"Yes, safe," Laura said, softly.

C.J. held out his hand. "Someplace safe," he said.

"Yes," she said and let him take the watch. Before he took a step away from the bed, the girl was asleep.

C.J. handed the watch to his father as they went to the door. Angus looked back at Laura and then left the girl alone with her mother.

The sharp whistle of a train sounded in the night, waking C.J. from a restless sleep. He lay there in the dark, wondering if it was real or whether it was from the dream he'd had. He vaguely remembered that it had something to do with a train and a bridge, but the memory was fading fast.

Then he heard another sound. There was a creak of the floor out in the hallway. He quietly got out of bed and quickly dressed, trying not to disturb Scotty, who was snoring away across the room. He went to the door and opened it.

Sadie was standing outside the door with her hand up, ready to knock.

"What are you doing?" C.J. whispered.

Sadie looked both ways in the hallway and then quickly stepped into C.J.'s room. "Laura's not in her bed," Sadie told him. "I heard the door shut, and she was gone."

"Maybe she went out to the privy," C.J. suggested.

"Maybe," Sadie said. "She was acting strange when we came back."

"She's been acting strange ever since she saw that watch," C.J. told her.

"I think we need to look for her and make sure she's OK." Sadie said.

C.J. agreed. They went down the back stairway to the kitchen. Sadie went out to the privy while C.J. waited for her. When she came back, she shook her head. They hurried into the front part of the house.

As they passed the front parlor, they noticed that out in the entry, the front door was wide open.

"Did she go outside?" C.J. asked.

"Where would she be going?" Sadie asked.

C.J. had an idea. He hurried to the study across the hall from the front parlor that his father was using for an office. He quickly found the cash box that his father used for a safe. Someone had pried the lid open with a knife. C.J. dug through the papers inside. The watch was gone.

He went back to the front door. Sadie was waiting.

"She took the watch." C.J. told her.

"Why?" Sadie asked.

"There's something weird about that watch," C.J. said. "Come on, let's find her."

They ran down the steps and through the front yard. There was no sign of Laura. They went to the gate and found it hanging slightly open. They pulled it open and glanced up and down the street.

"Look," Sadie whispered, grabbing C.J.'s arm. She pointed up the street towards Elm Street. C.J. saw the figure of a girl walking along the street. The figure turned onto Elm Street and disappeared behind the building on the corner.

Sadie ran to catch up to Laura, with C.J. running close behind.

"Where do you think she's going?" Sadie asked.

As if in answer, the mournful sound of a train whistle echoed through the small town.

When they reached the corner of Elm Street, they tried to find the girl in the shadows as they ran up the street toward the museum and train station.

C.J. was the first to spot her at the end of Main Street near the train station. The station itself was closed and dark, but they could see her in the light that shined from behind it.

They pushed themselves harder and ran faster until they reached the station. As they neared it, they saw Laura disappear around the side, heading for the platform. When they rounded the corner and climbed the steps to the platform, they stopped in their tracks.

A train was waiting at the platform, lit up with a strange, glowing light. The whistle blew again, and a voice came from a shadowy figure silhouetted in the door of one car.

"Last boarding," the voice called.

C.J. could see along the top of each car were the words "Dakota & Western Express".

It was the Phantom Express, and Laura was about to get on board.

Chapter 5

C.J. and Sadie saw Laura heading over to the ghostly train. They rushed after her and grabbed her arms. She struggled to get free, but they held her back.

"Let me go!" she yelled.

"Stop it," Sadie said. "You can't get on the train."

"I want to," she insisted. "I have to."

"No, you don't," C.J. said.

Laura continued to struggle. Whatever was compelling her to get on the train had given her tremendous strength. C.J. didn't think that either of them would be able to restrain her alone.

"This train isn't for you," C.J. told Laura. "It's for—" he began. He didn't finish the thought. He wasn't sure who it was for. He was going to say ghosts, but he didn't want to say that word out loud.

Laura suddenly stopped struggling. They kept their grip on her in case she was trying to put them off guard. However, when they heard the footsteps of someone climbing down from the train and walking toward them, they realized why she had stopped.

They maintained their hold on Laura as they turned around to see a large man in a conductor's uniform behind them. C.J. noticed Laura still had the watch in her hand.

"Are you folks riding the train tonight?" the man asked. He had a long face topped with white hair that stuck out from his cap. He looked down at the three of them through his rectangular glasses.

"No, sir," C.J. replied. "We don't have tickets."

The man looked straight at Laura. "Do you have a ticket, young lady?"

"No," Sadie said, stepping between Laura and the man. "She doesn't have a ticket either."

He stared at them and then nodded. "Have a good night then," he said and returned to the train.

"I want to get on the train," Laura called out.

The conductor turned back to her and shook his head. "I'm sorry, Miss," he said. "You can't ride the train without a ticket." He grabbed the railing and climbed up to the platform at the back of the coach car. He leaned out from the platform and called out, "All aboard!"

The train sounded its whistle, and with a blast of steam that almost filled the platform, the train pulled away. As it made its way down the tracks, the strange glow that emanated from the train faded, and it soon disappeared into the darkness.

Once the train was gone, Laura no longer fought them. She stood, looking down at the watch in her hands. C.J. and Sadie took that opportunity to lead her off the platform and away from the train station.

They led her down Elm Street and then around the corner to the house. As they entered the house, they heard the whistle again as the train began climbing the bluff.

They closed up the house and helped Laura up to her room. C.J. left Sadie to help Laura into bed and returned to his own room. It was hot and stuffy. He went to the window and opened it up. In the distance, he could see the shadowy forms of the bridges.

There was a light knock on the door and C.J. opened it to find Sadie standing outside.

"Laura is asleep again," she told him.

"She seems to sleep a lot after whatever the watch does to her," C.J. said.

Sadie pulled something out of her pocket and held it out to C.J. "Put it in a safe place," she told him.

C.J. took the watch and hid it in his suitcase.

"Look," Sadie said, pointing out the window.

They saw a glow at the top of the bluff right about where the old bridge stood. As it disappeared over the ridge, they heard a shrill whistle followed by the screech of the brakes on the train. The horrifying sound of the train crashing down to the river echoed through the town for several minutes, followed by a tremendous explosion.

Then there was silence.

At breakfast the next morning, C.J. pushed the scrambled eggs around his plate with his fork. He had risen early so that he could return the watch to the cash box. He tried to bend the edge of the lid back into place so it would latch when he closed it, and it did. He hoped that when his father tried to unlock the box, it would unlatch again.

He looked over at Sadie, who was eating her eggs, but not much faster than he was. She glanced up at him and then quickly looked down at her plate again.

Frederick and Scotty shoveled the last bites of their breakfasts into their mouths. The adults were enjoying their meals and drinking the fresh brewed morning coffee.

"Uh, Dad?" C.J. asked, his voice cracking a bit.

"What is it, C.J.?" his father asked. He was reading over the notes from the previous day's search.

"Did you, uh, sleep OK?"

"Fine. Why?"

"Just wondering," C.J. poked at his eggs again.

Angus looked up at his son. "Any special reason?"

"No," C.J. said, "just wondering."

Angus shrugged and went back to his paperwork.

After a few minutes, C.J. glanced up at his dad again. "Uh, Dad?"

"Yes, C.J.?" Angus asked, not looking up.

"You didn't, uh, hear anything in the night, did you?" the boy asked.

"Hear anything? Like what?"

"A train whistle, maybe?" C.J. asked.

Angus looked up at his son and thought for a moment. "No, I didn't hear a train whistle. Although I'm sure trains go through here in the middle of the night."

"This train was different," C.J. said.

"What was different about it?"

"It went up to the old bridge," C.J. said. He stopped playing with his food and stared at his plate, waiting for his father's response.

"The old bridge?" Angus asked. "The tracks up there don't connect to the line anymore."

"I know."

"How could it go up there, then?"

"Because it was the Phantom Express," C.J. said.

Everyone stopped what he or she was doing and listened.

"You heard the Phantom Express?" Angus asked.

C.J. nodded. "And, I saw it." He looked up at his dad and saw everyone looking at him. "Sadie saw it too," he said, pointing at her across the table.

Sadie blushed at the sudden attention. She nodded, but said nothing.

"And what did it do when it reached the old bridge?" Angus asked.

"It crashed," he said, and then added, "Again."

After his father insisted, C.J. told him about seeing the glowing train going up the slope to the old bridge and hearing the crash.

Sadie was relieved that he hadn't told them they followed Laura to the station and talked to the Phantom Express conductor. Her relief was short-lived, however.

"What was Sadie doing in your room in the middle of the night?" Edna asked. Although she had directed the question at C.J., she was looking squarely at Sadie.

"I woke up, and Laura was gone," she told her mother. "I went to get C.J.'s help in finding her."

"Where was Laura?" Teresa Hall asked, looking at her daughter.

"I don't remember being up," Laura said.

Sadie looked at C.J. for help.

"She went out back," he said. "We found her when she came back. She looked as if she were walking in her sleep. I'm not surprised she doesn't remember."

The adults quietly looked at the kids and tried to make up their minds about whether they believed them.

"Don't look at me," Scotty said. "I slept all night."

That was enough to break the tension in the room, and everyone relaxed. Edna told Angus that it was time to head out. He nodded.

"Let's talk about this Phantom Express later," he told C.J. "Right now, it's time to go."

"Can we ask Emerson about the watch?" C.J. asked.

The woman at the counter of the museum wore a plain blue dress and had her black hair up in a bun. She frowned at the kids as they entered.

"May I help you?" she asked, although it was obvious she wasn't happy that they were there.

"We are here to see Mr. Emerson," Sadie said. "The curator," she added when the woman looked at them like she didn't know what they were talking about. They stood as a group inside the door, far away from the counter.

She stared at them and then turned away. She knocked on a door behind the counter and waited.

They heard someone ask, "Yes?"

She opened the door and leaned in. After saying something they couldn't hear and getting an answer, she stood up straight again and closed the door. When she returned to her station, she said, "He will be with you in a moment."

They moved away from the door and stayed away from the woman behind the counter. She seemed to feel that she had dealt with them, so she went back to whatever it was she was doing when they first entered.

A few minutes later, the office door opened, and Eugene Emerson came out to greet them.

"What can I do for you, young people?" he asked tentatively, looking them over.

"I don't know if you remember us," C.J. said. "We were in here yesterday. Our parents are doing the excavation down at the river."

Emerson looked them over again. "Oh, yes," he said, becoming friendlier, "I remember. What can I do for you?"

"We found something out on the bridge yesterday, and we were wondering if you could help us with it?" C.J. asked.

"What did you find?"

"It was a watch," C.J. said, pulling it from his pocket, "a gold pocket watch. It was hanging from the bridge." He handed the watch to the curator.

The man took the watch and examined it inside and out. When he was done, he said, "Interesting."

"Do you think it's from the train?" Scotty asked.

"It's the right style, and the picture seems the proper age," the man told him.

"My dad thought so too," C.J. said.

"And you found it on the trestle?" Emerson asked.

"Yes," Laura said.

"Let's check a list of the passengers and crew for the train," the curator said. "Come with me."

They went inside the museum exhibit hall and headed for a shelf of books. The curator ran his finger across the bindings as he looked for the one he wanted, and with a cry of discovery, he pulled a red-bound book off the shelf.

He placed the book on the desk next to the bookshelf and opened it. After paging through it, he stopped on a particular page.

"Yes, here it is," he said. "A list of the passengers and crew of the Express in August 1883."

The Young Explorers gathered around him, trying to see the page that he was pointing to.

"Here's a possibility," Emerson said, "Calvin Olson. He could be the Cal inscribed on the watch."

"Was he a passenger?" Frederick asked.

"No, he was the conductor."

Sadie and C.J. looked at each other.

"I think we have a picture of him somewhere here," the curator said and looked through a wall of photographs. After a few moments, C.J. pointed to a picture of the crew of the Dakota & Western Express. His finger was on a large man with white hair and rectangular glasses.

"That was him," C.J. whispered. Sadie nodded.

"What did you say?" the curator asked.

"I said, that must be him," C.J. said, louder.

Emerson studied the picture. "Yes, it is," he said.

They continued to look through the pictures on the wall. There were pictures of the bridge after the crash, pictures of barges laden with pieces of the wreckage on a river that was much higher than the little stream that was left by the drought and pictures of the townspeople watching the recovery of bodies.

C.J. stopped to peer at one picture that showed several people standing on the bluff at the top of the bridge. He waved the others over.

"Does that look like the man we saw yesterday?" he asked them.

They all agreed that it did.

"Mr. Emerson," C.J. called to the curator, who was looking at some pictures at the other end.

"What is it?" he asked and strolled back to where the kids were standing.

"Was this the first mayor of Danford?" C.J. asked.

"Why, yes it is," Emerson said. "He was much older when I first met him. That would be him thirty years ago."

C.J. pointed to a young man standing next to the mayor. He looked much like Mayor Danford. "Then this would be his son, the current mayor of Danford." C.J. said.

"Yes," the curator said, "why?"

"He said he was out of town when the train crashed," C.J. said. "This picture shows he was right there."

Chapter 6

They looked closely at the framed photograph that contradicted the mayor's story about being out of town at the time of the train wreck.

The caption under the photograph said that a newspaper photographer from the Minneapolis Tribune had taken it the morning after the train wreck. In the picture, the mayor of Danford stood on the bluff by the collapsed bridge, overseeing the recovery of bodies from the river.

After the description was a list of other people pictured. They included Sheriff Fenn, Deputies Pierce and Kalb, Danford Station Master Monty Devin, and the mayor's son, Jefferson Danford, Jr.

"Why would he lie about being here?" Sadie asked. "Somebody would have remembered seeing him."

"Maybe," the curator said, "and then again, maybe not. The crash was the center of everyone's attention, not who was there and who wasn't."

"What about the picture?" C.J. asked.

"That was from a newspaper in Minneapolis," Emerson said. He unlocked a drawer in a cabinet below the pictures and pulled out a newspaper. "I doubt many people in Danford would have seen it."

On the front page of the newspaper above the picture was the headline, "Dakota Train Wreck".

"Still, why would he lie?" Sadie asked again.

"He's a junior," Emerson said, putting the newspaper back in the drawer and locking it again. "Many people named after their father were nervous during the trial. The search for Junior was almost like a witch hunt."

"Did they ever think he was Junior?" Scotty asked.

"I'm sure they did," he told them. "They investigated anyone nicknamed Junior."

C.J. looked at a picture of the gallows built to hang the three murderers. "They never found Junior?"

"They never could prove that anyone was the Junior," Emerson said. "I believe there is still a warrant for his arrest, but there hasn't been an active search for over 20 years."

C.J. looked again at the picture of the young man who would be mayor after his father. "What if he was Junior?"

The curator looked over the boy's shoulder. "If they could have proved he was Junior, he would have been arrested."

Sadie looked up from a diorama of the river gorge. "What would happen to Junior if they caught him?"

"They would try him for murder," Emerson said.

"Would they hang him?" Frederick asked.

"No," the curator said, "the state of North Dakota abolished the death penalty two years ago. If they found him guilty, he'd go to jail."

"Who would go to jail?" someone asked.

They looked up to find Henry Penn leaning against the doorframe with his arms crossed.

Emerson cleared his throat. "Well, Mr. Penn. We were just talking about Junior."

"I see," Henry said. He went to the wall of photos and glanced through a few. "Have any suspects?"

"The mayor," C.J. said quietly.

Henry frowned at C.J. "Why would you say that?"

The curator pulled C.J. back and stepped between them. "He's not saying that Mayor Danford is Junior," he said. "He just has a question about an inconsistency in the mayor's story."

"Inconsistency?" Henry asked.

"He said he wasn't here, but he was," C.J. told him.

"That doesn't mean he's Junior," Henry said. "He's a 'Junior', but not the one from the gang."

"What if he is?" Sadie asked. "What if a murderer is the mayor of Danford?"

Henry sat down on a bench. "We wouldn't want that," Henry agreed. "There isn't any proof."

"He lied," Laura said.

"So he lied about being here," Henry said. "I'd lie too if I were him. The search for Junior was a dark chapter in the history of this town. They questioned people for any reason, real or imagined."

"If he were Junior," Sadie said, "I think we should bring him to justice."

"What would that do after all these years?" Henry asked. "Would it bring all those people back?"

"Many people died because of him," C.J. said.

"I know," Henry said. "And Danford has spent his life trying to make this town more prosperous. If he were Junior, what good would it do to accuse him?"

"There would be justice for the dead," Sadie said.

"Maybe," Henry said. He looked out the window at the tracks running behind the building. "It would also mean opening old wounds and disgracing a man who dedicated his life to this town."

"You're running against him," Scotty said.

"I think he's been a fine mayor and done a wonderful job for this town," Henry said. "That doesn't mean that I don't think I can do even more for Danford's future."

He smiled at them. The smile didn't last long.

"No," he said, "making accusations against Mayor Danford, especially ones that aren't backed by proof, won't bring back the dead or improve anyone's life."

"But—," C.J. said.

"No, I want you to forget all about this," Henry told him. "Punishing someone for something done a long time ago when they were probably just a foolish, frightened boy will cause more suffering than good."

He stood up and stared hard at all the kids. "Don't mention these suspicions to anyone. Bury it and leave it buried, for this town's sake."

No one spoke or moved for a few moments.

Then Henry turned. "Mr. Emerson," he said, and nodded his head to the curator.

"Mr. Penn," Emerson said.

And then the mayoral candidate left the building.

Everyone looked around at the displays without a word for a few minutes. Finally, C.J. broke the silence. "Mr. Emerson, we should probably go down to the river and meet up with our parents."

"That might be a good idea," the curator said.

"Is there any way we could get a ride down there?"

Mr. Emerson thought for a moment. "Wait here," he said and went to the museum's front entrance.

The kids sat down to wait. None of them spoke, and most of them stared at the floor.

Finally, the curator returned. "It's a little rustic, but I found you a ride."

The rustic ride that Mr. Emerson found them turned out to be two magnificent, black Percheron horses pulling a wagon. The owner of the wagon was an older man named Peterson. He was a farmer who had several sections of land on the other side of the river. He was happy to give them a ride to the bridge.

As the farmer was pulling the wagon up to the front of the museum, the curator asked, "Would it be ok to hold on to the watch here at the museum?"

"That might be best," C.J. said with a glance over at Laura. She was looking at the horses and hadn't heard the curator's question.

"Thank you," the curator said. "Enjoy your ride."

The kids hopped up into the wagon and sat down on the bit of straw that was strewn about the bottom. They grabbed onto whatever they could when the horses started off and the wagon wobbled over the uneven road toward the river.

"What are you going to do?" Sadie asked C.J.

"I don't know," C.J. said. "I still think Junior should be punished even after so many years."

The heat of the afternoon beat down on them and made the straw hot. In fact, the straw wasn't just hot. It reeked. C.J. looked at Sadie and waved a hand in front of his nose.

"I know," Sadie said, wrinkling her nose in disgust.

"What if?" Laura said and stopped.

"What if what?" Scotty asked.

"What if the train wants him punished?" Laura asked. "What if that's what the train is waiting for?"

"That's dumb," Frederick said. "It's a train."

"A ghost train," Scotty said. "If you can believe in a ghost train, why couldn't you believe a ghost train keeps coming back for a reason?"

"You mean if we bring Junior to justice," C.J. said, "the train will stop crashing?"

"Why not?" Laura asked.

"That still leaves us where we were," C.J. said. "The mayor could be Junior, but we have no proof."

"How do we find proof, then?" Sadie asked.

"Maybe our parents would know how," C.J. said.

By the time Mr. Peterson dropped them off by the bridge, all the kids were glad to get out of the wagon. They all thanked the farmer and waved as he shook the reins and clicked at the horses to get them moving. Once he was out on the bridge and out of earshot, they stretched and groaned as they worked the aches out of their backs and legs.

"I'm never going to ride in a wagon again," C.J. said. Everyone murmured his or her agreement.

When they recovered, they made their way down to the beach and out onto the dry river bed to the team's archaeological site below the old train trestle.

Jackson Hall and Walter MacGregor were the only ones digging in the riverbed. They greeted the kids and told them that the rest of the crew was inside taking a break from the sun.

C.J. also noticed that there were some changes at the site since he'd left the day before. Several small white flags were stuck in the ground in various places around the site. Each flag had a number on it. They all knew that each flag showed they found something of interest there. They logged that number and a description of the object in their notes.

"Let's go see what they've found," C.J. said and ran to the tent. Everyone hurried after him.

Inside the tent, most of the adults were sitting in the shade and resting with a canteen of water. A long folding table covered with several artifacts was along one side of the tent. Attached to each one was a numbered tag.

After a quick hello, the kids walked the length of the table, looking to see what they had found. Some were common objects that were found in almost any river, like coins, broken bottles, and tin cans. Others were more unusual, like a silver spoon, a yarn doll, and a set of keys.

There were also a few articles on the table that made the kids think about the people who lost their lives in the train wreck. There were a pair of glasses, a brown leather shoe and the remains of a fancy woman's hat, with the remains of a feather matted down against the fabric.

C.J. looked around the table. "Where's the purse you found yesterday?" he asked his dad, who was sitting at the end of the table.

Angus nodded his head toward the other end of the tent. "Teresa is cleaning it over there," he said.

Teresa Hall was at a small table looking through a magnifying glass mounted on a stand so that she could examine objects while keeping both hands free. She was looking at a mesh purse and brushing it delicately with a small tool similar to a paintbrush.

Angus joined them and stood behind the kids as they watched her work. "Although it is dry now, the purse has been underwater for many years," he told them. "We have to be careful it doesn't fall apart."

"Dad," C.J. said quietly so as not to disturb Mrs. Hall, "can I ask you something?"

"Not right now," Angus said, still watching her work with the purse. "I think we're about to find out what's inside the purse."

C.J. looked back at the table to see Laura's mom carefully opening the latch on the purse. The two knobs on the latch moved slowly as she eased them apart. With a soft metallic click, the knobs snapped past each other and the curved metal pieces that sealed the top of the purse separated slightly.

Slowly, Teresa Hall opened the top of the purse wider. She picked up tweezers and slid it through the opening. She carefully worked one tine of the tweezers under something inside and then squeezed them together. She didn't pull it out immediately. She slowly put pressure on it to test whether is would separate from the sides of the purse.

"If she pulls too hard," Angus told the kids in a low voice, "it might rip apart."

The contents separated from the sides of the purse cleanly, and Teresa slid them out onto the table. She examined the inside of the purse again and discovered another small piece of paper. She repeated the procedure to remove that, as well.

As they carefully separated the contents of the purse into individual items, they discovered it contained a monogrammed handkerchief, several pieces of old paper money, a comb, and a compact.

When C.J. asked her about the other piece of paper, Teresa held it under the glass to examine it.

"This is interesting," she said. "It's a train ticket."

C.J. exchanged excited glances with Sadie. "Is it from the train crash?" he asked.

"It is a Dakota & Western Express ticket," she said. "That's not much of a surprise. That was the only train that went through here until recently." She examined the date.

C.J. barely contained his impatience.

"August 10, 1883," she read. "That matches the day the Dakota & Western Express crashed."

C.J. looked at the ticket over Teresa's shoulder. He couldn't contain his excitement any longer. He said, "You found a ticket for the Phantom Express."

Chapter 7

Angus took the ticket from Teresa. Enough of the faded printing remained so that the words were legible. Teresa moved out of the way so that he could look at it under the magnifying glass.

He examined the paper, the ink, and the style of railroad logo that appeared along the top edge of the ticket. "Hmm," he said, "looks right." To the others, he said, "We'll have to compare it to other tickets used by the railroad. I'd say it is genuine."

"If it is a ticket for the Express, that means the purse was from the train wreck," C.J. exclaimed.

Angus continued to examine the paper. He ran his finger along the edge. A used ticket normally would have a hole punched into it along the edge. The hole could have closed up as the water expanded the paper, but Angus saw no sign of a punch.

Finally, he looked up. "It seems so," he said. "The conductor didn't punch this ticket." He moved to the side and held the ticket so that the others could take turns looking through the magnifying glass.

Sadie took her turn when C.J. was done. He looked at the myriad of artifacts laid out on the table. "Are all the rest of these from the accident?" he asked.

"No," his father told him. "The ticket might show the purse and everything in it was from the train. Most of the others were thrown into the river or accidentally dropped from a passing boat."

"Everything else will have to be examined and evaluated individually," Teresa told him.

When everyone had seen the ticket, Angus set it back on the worktable.

Teresa placed the purse and its contents in a bag, sealed it and placed the bag in a storage bin until they could move it offsite. She went over to the table and, after looking through the artifacts, picked up the doll to examine next.

Sadie nudged C.J. with her elbow and nodded at his dad. C.J. frowned at her and elbowed her back. He stepped closer to his dad and cleared his throat.

"Uh, Dad?" C.J. said.

"Hmm?" Angus said. He looked through the magnifying glass over Teresa's shoulder while she examined the strands of yarn that made up the doll's hair.

"We have a question," C.J. said.

"What is it?" Angus said, watching the cleaning.

"You know Junior of the train gang?" C.J. asked.

"Not personally," Angus joked. "I know who you're talking about."

"What if we think we know who he is?" C.J. asked. "Should we report him?"

Angus turned and gave C.J. his full attention. "I suppose so," he said. "Why? Do you know who it is?"

C.J. looked at the other kids. They nodded at him.

"I think," he began, "I mean, we think Mayor Danford is the Junior from the Penny Ante Gang."

Angus narrowed his eyes at his son. "Really? Why do you think that?"

"Well, they named him after his dad. So he is a junior," C.J. said. "And you know how he said that he was at school when the train crashed?"

"I remember," Angus said. He sat down on one of the folding chairs.

C.J. sat down in a chair facing him. "There's a picture of him with his dad by the bridge on the morning after the crash," he said.

"OK," Angus said. He sat back and waited for his son to continue with his evidence.

"That's it," C.J. said.

"He is a junior, and he was here that morning," Angus said, summing up C.J.'s argument. "That's all?"

C.J. stood up again. "Isn't that enough?" he asked.

"No," Angus said. "That isn't proof he's Junior. It only means there is a possibility he could be Junior."

"If he is, we should bring him to justice," C.J. said.

Angus waved his hand at the chair. C.J. sat down.

"Yes, if he is Junior, we should bring him to justice," Angus told him. "It isn't enough to accuse him. If he is innocent and you accuse him of this, it could ruin his life."

C.J. flopped back in the chair and folded his arms over his chest. He didn't look at his dad.

"Unless you find more evidence, I suggest you drop it," Angus told him.

"But dad," C.J. said.

Angus stood up. "I think that you Young Explorers have had far too much time on your hands," he said. "You need something more constructive to do."

Over the next few minutes, Angus assigned jobs to each of the kids. Laura would help her mother, Teresa, and learn how to clean artifacts. Sadie's job was to help her dad, Walter, find artifacts in the compacted soil of the dry riverbed. He assigned Frederick to Edna MacGregor to learn how to catalog the artifacts. And Scotty would help Angus with his projects.

Only C.J. did not have a job.

"I have a special assignment for you," Angus told his son. "We've taken several photographs of the area. You can go back to the house with Mr. Hall, set up a dark room, and develop those pictures."

After calling Jackson into the tent, Angus saw that C.J. was looking at a camera. "Do you think you can handle that?" he asked.

"I can handle it," C.J. said. He tried to hide his excitement about it. He looked forward to learning how to develop photographs.

When Angus told Jackson what he had in mind for C.J. and him, Jackson readily agreed.

"Come on, sport," Jackson said to C.J. "Let's load up the film and see what we can develop."

They loaded up a box with the film to process and headed out across the riverbed, back to the beach.

When they arrived back at the house, they found Mrs. Wesley in the parlor, working on her cross-stitching by the dim light of a small lamp. All the drapes had been closed throughout the main floor, and the house was dark.

"Sorry, Mrs. Wesley," Jackson said. "We didn't mean to interrupt your needlework."

"No need for an apology, Mr. Hall," Mrs. Wesley said. She laid her cross-stitch in her lap. "I'm making a little something for my granddaughter."

"You should open the drapes," C.J. suggested. "You'd be able to see better."

"No," she said, "I like the cool darkness of the house on a hot day like today."

Jackson excused himself to gather the photo equipment he would need to set up the darkroom and suggested that C.J. sit with Mrs. Wesley for a moment until he returned.

C.J. sat down, and neither one said anything. Finally, C.J. broke the silence. "We're going to set up a darkroom in the cellar so that we can develop some photographs that we've taken down by the river."

"Oh," Mrs. Wesley said, "photographs? Really?"

"Yes, Ma'am," C.J. said.

Mrs. Wesley leaned back in her chair in the shadows. For a moment, it seemed as if she had fallen asleep. Then, in a soft voice, she said, "I think photographs are amazing. We had nothing like that when I was a little girl."

Before C.J. could say anything, Jackson returned to the parlor carrying a large bag similar to what a doctor usually carried when making a house call.

"You ready?" Jackson asked C.J.

C.J. stood to follow Jackson to the cellar.

Jackson turned to the woman. "If you don't mind, Ma'am," Jackson said, "we would like to use some space in the cellar to develop some photographs."

"I don't mind at all, Mr. Hall," Mrs. Wesley said.

Jackson thanked the woman. They headed to the cellar and stopped when the woman called to them.

"Yes, Ma'am?" Jackson asked.

"Would it be possible to see some of your pictures when you are done?" she asked.

"Certainly, Ma'am," Jackson said. "I'd be happy to show them to you."

The cellar had no electricity. They found a supply of candles and matches at the top of the steps leading into the dank and musty space under the house. The flickering candles did little to cast light about the room but caused objects there to cast shadows into the corners.

Besides shelves stacked with preserves, the cellar contained a worktable, several replacement windows and doors leaning against one wall, and a monstrous furnace that filled one corner of the room.

In the winter, furnaces would have a life of their own with the heat and light of the coal fire within it. Furnaces like that were enough to keep children too scared to go into the cellar. Since it was summer though, the furnace was a cold, lifeless, metal box.

Jackson set his candle and bag on the table. Next to the table, a spigot jutted out of the wall over a floor drain. He turned the water on for a moment and checked it. "That'll do," he said and turned it off.

The man returned to the table and opened the bag. C.J. stood beside him and tried to see what he had in it.

Jackson set four metal pans in a row on the table. Next to the first three pans, he placed a stoppered bottle. Each bottle had a chemical solution in it.

Then, he set out a box with colored sides, four film reels, a stopwatch, tongs, a ball of twine, scissors, and some small wood pins similar to clothes pins.

Jackson gave the twine and scissors to C.J. and had him tie two lines for hanging the photographs to dry after they processed them. He then attached the pins to the lines so that they were ready to hold the finished pictures.

Jackson poured the liquid from one bottle into the first pan. He repeated that with the other two bottles. He placed the film from the camera next to the first of the pans and set the stopwatch.

"I have to transfer the film into the developer solutions," he told C.J. "That has to be done in total darkness so that we don't ruin the film."

With that, he blew out both candles and started his work. C.J. stood by and stayed out of his way.

"To develop the film," Jackson explained to him in the dark, "it has to be put in a developer solution."

C.J. heard the man place the film in one pan. For several minutes, he heard the liquid sloshing around in the pan.

"That part is done," Jackson told him. "Hold on, I'll get a light going."

C.J. heard him moving something around on the table and then the sound of a match. Instead of the flare of a match lighting a candle, a dim glow came from the box with colored sides. The box covered the candle and only let out a dull red light.

"It's a safelight," Jackson said. "We can still damage the film with too much light. This allows us to see without ruining the pictures."

C.J. saw Jackson place the film into the second of the two pans of chemical solutions with a set of tongs.

"The second step is called the stop bath," Jackson told him. "This neutralizes the developer chemicals and halts further developing."

After several seconds of swishing the solutions over the film, he lifted the reels out with the tongs and let the solutions drip off of it.

He then set them into the third pan and set the stopwatch going. As the time ticked away, he swished the fluid over the film.

"This is the final step," Jackson said. "It's called the fixer. It stabilizes the image and makes it insensitive to light. If we didn't do this step, the photo would darken and fog."

They waited for several minutes as he continued to swish the chemical solution over the reels of film.

He then took each reel and ran a slow stream of water over it from the spigot for several minutes. Once he thoroughly rinsed each reel, he set them on the table and showed C.J. how to remove the film from the reels.

Soon, they had the reels removed from each roll of film. Jackson placed a weight on the end of each roll and handed it to C.J. who hung it on the drying lines.

Once that was done, Jackson pulled the safelight box off of the candle so they could see their work.

C.J. saw the things hanging on the line weren't photos. They were small, and it was hard to see an image on it.

Jackson saw C.J.'s confusion. "They're negatives," he said. "Once they're dry, we can create the photos."

Over the next few hours, they took each of the negatives and exposed it to a sheet of photo paper.

They ran each photograph through the developer solution, the stop bath, and then the fixer solution. Again, once they rinsed the photographs thoroughly, they hung them on the line to dry.

By the time the afternoon drew to a close, they'd developed two dozen photos.

C.J. glanced through the pictures. On one of them, Sadie seemed blurry, but everyone else seemed clear.

"She probably moved during the exposure," Jackson said. "The exposure is determined by how long you hold down the exposure button. The longer the exposure, the more likely someone is to move."

He pointed out Laura's eyes in the same photo. They appeared ghostly. "She blinked," he said.

C.J. looked through the other pictures. Most were pictures taken of the dig site where they found and partly uncovered some artifacts. Others showed the bridge and other parts of the riverbed.

Finally, he found the ones that he and his friends had taken. The pictures weren't half bad. He looked at them in the order they had taken them. The first was at the bottom of the bridge and then each of the others as they climbed to the top. At the end of the line of photos, he found the one that was taken looking out across the bridge.

He stopped and looked closer at the photograph, bringing the candle near it to see.

He saw a blurred figure out on the bridge.

"What's this?" C.J. asked.

Jackson looked at the photo where C.J. pointed. "Was that when Laura walked out there?" he asked.

"No, I took this before that happened. We had just gotten up there." C.J. said.

Jackson went to his bag and pulled out a magnifying glass and held it over the photo. He studied the picture for a moment and then said, "It looks like a man was standing out there."

He gave C.J. the magnifying glass to look again. "You didn't see anyone out there?" he asked the boy.

"No," C.J. said and looked at the figure through the glass. It was definitely the figure of a man, and although it appeared ghostly like someone who moved during the exposure, C.J. recognized the man.

It was the conductor of the Phantom Express.

Chapter 8

"That's the conductor from the Express," C.J. said. "Here, look." He handed the magnifying glass back to Jackson.

Jackson studied the image. He moved the candle closer to get more light on it. "Are you sure?" he asked. "It could be a flaw in the developing." He went to the line of photos and located the negative. He inspected the original image to see if it also contained the figure.

"I saw the conductor," C.J. said. "It's him."

"You saw the conductor?" Jackson glanced up.

C.J. realized his mistake. "I saw a picture of him," he said, "in the museum."

"It could be your imagination," Jackson said. "More likely it's just a flaw in the film."

"He's not," C.J. said. "It's the ghost of the conductor. It looks like him."

"A ghost?" Jackson raised an eyebrow.

"Yes," C.J. said. He didn't meet Jackson's gaze. "A ghost," he repeated.

"Why would his ghost be in one of your pictures?" Jackson asked, examining the picture again.

C.J. looked at the picture and thought for a moment. Then he snapped his fingers. "The watch," he said. "That's where we found his gold watch."

Jackson looked at the photo again and was quiet for a moment. "I don't know," he said.

"I know," a woman said close behind them.

Both of them jumped and turned to find Mrs. Wesley was standing behind them in the shadows of the cellar.

"You startled me," Jackson said.

"Me, too," C.J. added.

"We didn't hear you come down," Jackson said.

"I'm sorry," Mrs. Wesley said. "I guess someone appearing out of the darkness would startle me, too."

"That's all right," Jackson said. "You said that you knew who this man was?"

"The young man is correct," she said. "It's Calvin Olson, the conductor on the Express."

"Are you sure?" Jackson asked. "Do you need to look closer at it?"

"Oh, no," she told him. "I saw him many times on the train. He's the conductor."

Jackson examined the photo with the glass.

"You don't believe me?" she asked.

"It's not that," he said. "It's the idea that we have a ghost in one of our pictures is..."

"Is what?" the woman asked, smiling.

"It's hard to believe," he told her.

"You don't believe in ghosts," she said. It was a statement rather than a question.

"Oh, I do," Jackson said. "We saw one in Peru."

"There are ghosts everywhere," the old woman said, "some real, some memories."

Jackson put the picture down. "Well, C.J.," he said, "I suppose we should pack up our equipment and take these photos down to the others."

He and C.J. began packing up the bag.

"Thank you for the use of your cellar," Jackson said, turning to the old woman. She was gone.

He glanced around the shadows of the basement, shook his head, and went back to work.

On the way back to the river, C.J. opened the folder and pulled out the photograph. He checked the conductor's ghostly image again.

"Why do you think he was there?" C.J. asked.

Jackson sped up along the road leading out of town. "Maybe that's where he died?"

"Maybe," C.J. said. He tried to find where the watch had been hanging. There was no sign of it.

"Maybe he wanted us to find the watch," C.J. said.

"If he's a ghost," Jackson said, "why would that matter to him?"

"I don't know," C.J. said.

Jackson turned onto the road to the beach. "You'd better put it away before dust ruins it," he told him.

When the Packard stopped, C.J. grabbed the binder and practically ran down the beach and slid down the embankment to the riverbed.

"Careful there," Jackson called to him.

C.J. was back on his feet and running to the tents.

"We have the pictures," the boy called to Walter and Sadie, who were patiently carving away the hardened clay of the riverbed. "Come see them."

Without stopping to see if they were going to follow him, C.J. burst into the tent. Everyone turned to see what all the excitement was about. "Here are the pictures," he told them between breaths.

"Why all the excitement?" Angus asked, taking the binder from his son.

"It's a surprise," C.J. said. "Look at them."

Angus narrowed his eyes at his son. He opened the binder and removed the photos.

Everyone gathered around to see them.

By the time Walter and Sadie entered the tent, finally followed by Jackson, the photos were being passed from person to person.

"You took some good pictures," Angus said.

"They certainly did," Edna agreed.

"Wait until you see the last one," C.J. said.

When Angus reached the one at the top of the bridge, he stopped and squinted at the figure hovering over the tracks. "What is this?"

Angus held it under the magnifying glass with plenty of light to study the image.

"It's a ghost," C.J. said.

Many of the adults chuckled at his words while the kids gathered around his father and tried to get a look at the ghost in the photo.

"It's definitely a figure," Angus said. "An after image of another exposure?" He looked at Jackson.

"Not that I can see," Jackson said. "C.J. says it's the conductor from the Express."

Angus looked up at his son.

"It is," Sadie said. "I recognize him from the..." She stopped suddenly, realizing that she was going to say that she saw him at the station.

"From where?" Edna asked her daughter.

"From a picture in the museum," C.J. said.

"What do you think?" Angus asked Jackson.

"Well, Mrs. Wesley agreed with C.J.," Jackson said. "And she actually saw him."

"Interesting," Angus said. "We'll have to compare it to the photograph at the museum."

"I think it's the watch," C.J. said. "He's standing where we found it."

Angus glanced at Laura, who pushed through the other kids to get a better look.

Angus looked to C.J. and caught his eye. He nodded toward Laura and held a finger to his lips. C.J. didn't know what he wanted.

"Interesting theory," Angus said. "We'll have to look at this a little closer." He glanced at his watch. "It will have to wait until later. Right now, I think it's time to pack up what we've found and take it all up to the museum."

Without another word, the adults went to work wrapping the last of the artifacts and carefully packing them in containers.

As the kids jumped in to help, Angus drew C.J. aside. "If there is a ghost involved with the watch," he whispered to his son, "it may be best not to talk about it around Laura."

C.J. nodded and went to help pack up.

After the containers were ready, the group closed up the tent and carried the artifacts up to the beach and the waiting vehicles.

By the time the caravan arrived back in town and pulled up in front of the museum, the sun had set, and darkness had fallen on Danford.

The museum wasn't the only building lit up for the night. Lights were on at the train depot and a large crowd gathered in front of it.

A banner across the street side of the building announced that a debate between the mayoral candidates was taking place.

On a lighted platform set in front of the building, Jefferson Danford, Jr. and Henry Penn were addressing the audience and each other with voices alternately rising and then fading again as they were cheered and booed by the crowds.

Angus nudged C.J., who had stopped to watch the debate. C.J. picked up a container and followed the others into the lobby of the museum.

The curator hurried out of his office as soon as the receptionist told him they had arrived.

With an exclamation of excitement, he opened the door into the museum's main room and cleared space on one of the display cases for the new artifacts.

They placed all the containers on the table and removed the artifacts, placing them gently on the glass of the display case.

"Oh my," the curator said as he looked over the items, "it is so wonderful that you have found such interesting objects. It gives us a connection with the past and, in this case, with the people who lost their lives on the train."

The curator looked over the individual items, skipping past cans and bottles. He stopped at the doll.

"Do you know what may have come from the Express?" he asked, touching the yarn hair.

"Some of it did," Angus said. "But we'll have to do some more research."

"There's a ticket for the Express," C.J. said.

The curator perked up at that news. "Where?"

C.J. pointed out the purse and the ticket beside it.

"Do you have an example of a ticket for the Express that we can compare it to?" Angus asked.

"Certainly," the curator said. He went to a display case next to the wall of photos and lifted the top. He plucked out a ticket and replaced the lid.

"It's not for the doomed train itself," he said. "It's from the same year, though."

Angus took it and compared the two. Except for the faded ink of the waterlogged one, they matched.

He put them both on the table and said, "It looks like it could be a genuine ticket."

"What ticket would that be?" someone asked from the museum door.

Mayor Danford and Henry Penn stood in the doorway watching them.

"A ticket for the Express," the curator said. "They found one in a purse from the river."

The mayor moved to the display and glanced at the items scattered across its top. Mr. Penn pushed between him and the curator so he could see.

"Interesting," the mayor said, picking up the ticket. "For the Express, you say?"

"Yes," the curator said, "and they also found this gold pocket watch." He held up the pocket watch for them to see.

The mayor dropped the ticket back on the table and took the watch from the curator.

C.J. watched the mayor as the man examined the pocket watch. He opened it and looked at the picture. He didn't look behind it at the inscription.

After a moment, the man snapped it shut and handed it back to the curator. "Very nice," he said.

"They found this watch on the bridge. It may have belonged to the conductor who died in the crash," the curator said. "It has a picture of his wife inside."

"Really?" the mayor said. "That is interesting."

Henry reached for the watch, but the mayor suddenly snatched it back from the curator.

"Who's that?" the mayor asked when he opened the watch again and looked closer at the photo inside.

"It's his wife," Henry Penn said as he picked up the forgotten ticket and looked it over.

"How would I have known that?" the mayor asked. "I'm not psychic." He handed the gold watch back to the curator.

"Listen to what people tell you," Henry told him. "Eugene said it was his wife." He moved around the table, looking through the other artifacts.

C.J. looked around the table, but the ticket wasn't there. Glancing around more, he saw Henry was still holding it as he looked around the table.

"What else did you find that's interesting?" the mayor asked, glancing around.

"The ticket," C.J. said.

"Oh yes," the mayor said. "You showed me a ticket earlier. What was so special about it?"

The curator began moving artifacts around, looking for the ticket. Finally, the mayor held it up. "Here it is," he said.

The curator took the ticket from him and looked at it. "This is the one we already had on display," he said. "Where is the other one?"

"Mr. Penn has it," C.J. said, pointing at the ticket still clutched in the man's hand.

"Oh, I'm sorry," Henry said. "I didn't realize that I was holding it." He handed it to the curator.

The man was glad to have it back in his hands. "This one was actually for the train that crashed." He showed the date to the mayor, who leaned in to see it.

C.J. looked at Henry Penn, who stared back at him.

The mayor sighed. "That was a sad chapter in the history of this town," he said. "My father, Jefferson Danford, Sr., who was mayor when it happened, took it hard." He put the ticket back on the table. "It weighed heavily on his mind," the current mayor continued. "He was never the same again."

The mayor pulled a handkerchief out of his pocket and dabbed at his eyes. Everyone silently waited.

"Thank you," he said when he had composed himself. "Thank you for helping us remember those who died in that tragic crash."

The mayor walked over to Angus and shook his hand, grasping Angus's hand with both of his.

"You don't have to thank us," Angus told him. "We are honored to do what we can."

He went from one to another, shaking their hands.

Then, the mayor looked around the table and said, "The more you find, the more this museum makes me feel as if I were there that day."

"You were there that day," C.J. said. Everyone turned to look at the young boy, who stood glaring at the mayor.

"C.J.," Angus snapped at him.

The mayor stood there, his mouth opening and closing, but not a word came out. Finally, his mouth snapped shut. "What do you mean?" he demanded.

"You were here that day," C.J. repeated. He went over to the pictures on the wall and pointed to the one showing him with his dad on the overlook. "Right there," he said.

The mayor looked at the photo, and his face turned white. "Why...I...," he said and then fell silent, staring at the picture.

"Why are you lying?" C.J. asked. "Are you Junior?"

Chapter 9

The mayor was visibly shaking as he stood there staring at the young boy, who dared to speak to him like that. "I...what...you," he stammered. He took a breath and composed himself.

"I don't have to stand here and have some little boy talk to me that way," he told C.J. "I am a prominent citizen of this great town and its mayor." He took a step closer to C.J. and looked down at him. "I am not some two-bit outlaw. So don't go accusing me of something that you can't back up with facts."

He glared at C.J., and his eyes narrowed at the boy.

C.J. stared right back at him. After a few moments of silence, C.J. said in a quiet, firm voice, "Then why did you lie about being in town that day?" When the mayor didn't answer right away, he continued. "You said you were off at boarding school," he pointed again at the picture on the wall. "Except you were right there by your father."

"Are you going to let him talk to me like that?" the mayor asked Angus.

"I'm not happy that he brought it up so publicly," Angus said, "But C.J. has a valid question."

The mayor glanced around at the faces, looking back at him, waiting for an answer. "Well," he said, "I am not Junior, and I was not a member of that gang."

He ran a hand through his hair and felt the sweat on his brow. He pulled a handkerchief from his pocket and mopped his forehead. "Ok, I was in town," he said, "and I was never at any boarding school."

"Why did you tell everyone that?" C.J. asked.

He glared at the boy. "I didn't, in the beginning." He sat down heavily in a chair next to the display of photos. "You don't know what it was like after the crash when it became known that there was another member of the gang on the loose, and his nickname was Junior."

He had a faraway look in his eyes as he remembered that time thirty years earlier. "It was like a witch hunt," he said. "They wanted someone to hang, and my father was afraid for my life. He didn't want his son railroaded to the gallows just because he named me after him."

He looked around at the faces of his audience again. "So he lied. He made up a story that I had gone off to boarding school. My grandfather had broken his arm that July and I spent a lot of time helping him at his farm outside of town. No one saw me here for a while. And, with all the commotion with the crash, no one paid any attention to if I was here. Nobody questioned the story."

He looked back at C.J. He was no longer angry. "Yes, I was here, and yes, my father and I lied about it. I am not Junior, and I was never part of the Penny Ante Gang."

The mayor stood up and went to the table where he stood looking through the artifacts in the awkward silence that followed his story. He pushed a few items around and picked up the ticket again.

Angus frowned at his son, yet said nothing to him. His look told C.J. there would be words later.

The mayor interrupted the silence. "Did you put him up to that?" he asked. He glared at Henry Penn. "Did you put those thoughts into his head so he could do your dirty work for you?"

"What are you talking about?" Henry asked.

"You want to discredit me," Jefferson said, waving the ticket at his mayoral opponent. "You put those thoughts into his head so that people would think I'm a criminal."

"I did not," Henry said.

"He didn't, Mayor Danford," C.J. said. "I saw the picture, and I remembered you said you weren't here. He actually told me not to bring it up."

"As did I," Angus said. "He acted according to his own conscience and not on anyone's behalf."

The mayor looked first from C.J. who nodded his agreement, to Angus, and then to Henry.

"I swear I did not put him up to it," Henry told him. He moved closer to the mayor and lowered his voice. "Jeff, I respect what you and your father did for this town," he said. "While I think Danford would benefit from my ideas as mayor, I would do nothing to discredit you personally, or your father's memory, to win the election."

The mayor stared at him. He opened his mouth as if he were going to speak, but said nothing.

Henry took the train ticket the mayor still held in his hand and then offered his hand to the man.

The mayor hesitated, then extended his hand and took Henry's. As they shook hands, the tension ebbed, and everyone breathed a collective sigh of relief.

Angus nudged C.J. He approached the mayor and interrupted the handshake. "I'm sorry I accused you of being Junior," he told the mayor.

Danford gave Henry's hand one last shake and turned to the boy. After giving C.J. a long look, the mayor said, "I accept your apology, young man."

C.J. nodded, and they shook hands. As C.J. let go of the mayor's hand and tried to turn to go, the mayor kept his grip on the boy's hand.

"Next time you want to accuse someone of something," Danford told him, "don't do it so publicly."

C.J. nodded, and the mayor let him go. C.J. went to the table and busied himself with looking through the artifacts and ignoring everyone else in the room.

No one else paid any attention to the table except for Henry Penn. He looked at the ticket that was still in his hand and then pushed it under some other papers on the table.

The mayor also watched what Henry was doing.

The curator glanced up at the clock on the wall. It was about half-past eight. "Ladies and gentlemen," he said to get the attention of the group, "it's after eight and I must close up the museum."

"Oh, of course," the mayor said. "I'm sorry that we've kept you from your duty." Despite the apology, he remained talking with Henry next to the pile of papers where Penn hid the ticket.

"Mr. Emerson," Angus called to the curator, "can we leave everything here and deal with it in the morning when the museum opens again?"

"That is agreeable to me," the curator said.

C.J. didn't want to leave yet. He waited for the two mayoral candidates to leave so that he could secure the ticket. Both men seemed overly interested in the ticket, and C.J. didn't want it to walk away.

Neither man moved from his position. Even when each wanted to thank his father and the team for their work, they called them over to where they were rather than leaving their place.

When he saw his father was going to leave before the two men, he decided he had to make his move to prevent them from taking the ticket.

He watched until he was sure no one was paying any attention to him and then ducked under the display case. He crept along the floor and moved to the edge where the men stood. The pile of papers hiding the ticket was directly above him.

From the positions of the men's feet, he saw they watched the rest getting ready to leave and had their backs to the table. He reached up around the edge of the table and carefully felt around for the pile of papers. In a matter of moments, he found the papers and slipped his hand under them, looking for the ticket.

The two men moved, and C.J. thought for a moment that they would catch him. Then his fingers found the edge of the ticket and he quickly pulled it out and down under the table.

He crept to the other end of the display case and pocketed the ticket before standing up and pretending that he had been standing there the whole time.

It was just in time. "C.J.," Angus called. He was looking around the room for him. "Where are you?" Then Angus spotted his son. "There you are. Come on, it's time to go."

He walked toward the door where his father stood and passed the candidates. He didn't look at them and kept walking.

At the door, he glanced back over his shoulder and saw the two men facing each other across the display case with the pile of papers between them. Why were they so interested in the ticket?

Everyone gathered on the street outside the museum and wished each other farewell. The curator and the two candidates headed back to their homes while the adults loaded up into the cars.

"Let's go," Walter called to the kids.

"Can we walk?" C.J. asked. "It was stuffy in there."

Walter looked at the other adults and, after a few nods, told them not to take too long.

The kids started walking along the wooden sidewalk that ran along the street on both sides and waved to the caravan as it passed.

Once the cars were out of sight, C.J. told the others about the candidates and their interest in the ticket.

"It's an old ticket," Scotty said. "Why would they be interested in that?"

"I don't know," C.J. told them. He hurried to catch up to Sadie and walked with her. "Do you have any ideas?" he asked her.

"No," she said, "what good is it to anyone?"

"You should have had the curator lock it up in his office," Frederick told him.

"It's probably too late now," Laura said. "They were the last ones to leave. Either of them could have taken it."

"They didn't take it," C.J. told them.

"How do you know?" Sadie asked.

"Because I have it," he said and produced the ticket to show them.

"How were you able to take it from under their noses?" Sadie asked.

Before he could tell them anything more, he heard a creak of a board from the sidewalk behind them.

He stopped and listened. Everyone else stopped and wondered what he was doing, everyone except for Frederick, who also listened.

"Did you hear that?" C.J. asked the older boy.

Frederick scanned the street behind them. Neither he nor C.J. could see anyone.

"Somebody's following us," Frederick whispered.

"I wish we'd gone with our parents," Laura said.

C.J. stepped closer to Frederick. "Which side are they on?" he whispered.

"Can't tell," Frederick said. "There are shadows on both sides." He glanced up at the moon, which was a sliver of light. "The moon is no help."

"We'd better move faster," C.J. said. They all started walking quickly along the sidewalk.

C.J. stayed with Frederick as they hurried down the street. "Can you hear anything?" C.J. asked him.

"Whoever it is," Frederick said, looking back, "they're keeping up with us, maybe getting closer."

"Do you think we'll make it home before they catch us?" C.J. asked.

Frederick glanced back again. "If they want that ticket," he told C.J., "I'd say no."

He looked ahead to Sadie and noticed that Scotty was not with her. "Where's your brother?" C.J. asked.

"He ran ahead," Sadie said. "We should all run."

"I agree," Frederick said, and they ran.

As soon as they ran, they heard the distinct sound of someone running on the sidewalk behind them. They were close to the turn onto First Avenue where the boarding house stood, but they were still a block from it.

Whoever was chasing them would catch them before they reached the house.

They rounded the corner and almost ran into Scotty. He stood by a door leading into the corner building, and it was open. He waved them in. "It was unlocked," he whispered.

C.J. followed them in and pushed the door closed until a soft click signaled it latched.

It was the back room of a blacksmith's shop. With the little light that filtered in through the door, they saw that a brick forge dominated the center of the room with dozens of tools lining the walls and lying on every surface of the room.

C.J. stood at the door with his hand on the knob and listened for their pursuer as the other four scattered about the room, looking for hiding places.

He heard footsteps outside and waited for the person to pass on down the street. When he felt the knob move in his hand, he jumped behind a nearby barrel to hide.

From the hiding places, they all heard the slight creak of the door as someone entered the shop. The door closed and someone stood there in the dark, breathing heavily from the run.

Slowly, the intruder moved around the forge, looking for them. After making a complete circuit around the forge and almost tripping over a stool, the figure stood by the door and listened again.

Then they heard a low, hoarse whisper that was just loud enough for everyone in the room to hear. "You need to stop asking about Junior," the person said. "As far as this town is concerned, Junior is gone, and I don't need you to bring him back."

The figure stood silently and listened again.

The whisper began again. "I want that ticket," it said. "Return that ticket to the museum by closing time tomorrow night or you might not live to see another day."

With that, the figure opened the door and left them alone in the dark room.

Chapter 10

There was no movement or sound inside the blacksmith's shop for quite a while after the man left. None of the kids was sure that he had actually gone, and no one wanted to risk leaving his or her hiding place to find out.

C.J.'s legs cramped as he kneeled behind the barrel. He wouldn't be able to stay there much longer. Plus, their parents would wonder where they were and come look for them, but they wouldn't have any reason to look for them in the blacksmith's shop. They had to get back out on the street.

C.J. used the barrel to pull himself up and let the blood flow back into his legs. He glanced around the dark room and saw nothing except the shadowy forge and the tools that were strewn about.

He moved toward the door, expecting the intruder to jump out at him. When he reached the door, he jumped back when he saw a shadowy figure beside it.

He was ready to run. A moment later, he relaxed and chuckled to himself. The figure was the blacksmith's leather apron hung on a post next to the door.

He took one last look around and, satisfied that the man was gone, called out softly to his friends. "You can come out now. He's gone."

Out of the darkness, a small figure appeared, and then another. Soon, five stood together by the door.

"My legs hurt," Scotty said. "I didn't think I'd be able to stand up again."

"I know what you mean," C.J. said.

"You had it easy," Frederick told them. "I was lying on the woodpile under the bench over there. One log had a sharp point that stuck me in the back the entire time." He stretched and rubbed his lower back.

"We'd better get back to the house," C.J. said. He turned the knob and eased the door open a crack.

The street outside looked deserted, so he opened the door wider and stuck his head out. He couldn't see anyone on the street.

"Let's go," he whispered and pulled the door open far enough for them to leave.

They filed out onto the street, glancing in every direction for any sign of movement.

The street was far brighter to them after their time in the almost total darkness of the blacksmith's shop. There was no one on the street waiting for them.

Jackson Hall took them by surprise as he came around the corner from Elm Street.

"Where have you five been?" he demanded.

After the fright that Jackson gave them passed, they just stared at him. They didn't know what to say.

"Let's not all talk at once," Jackson said. When no one volunteered an explanation, he said, "Oh, never mind. Let's get you back to the house."

They all followed him along the street until they reached the gate to the house. They felt better knowing Laura's dad was with them, yet they still kept watch for anyone else who might follow them.

When they reached the house, they hurried through the gate and took the porch steps two at a time. Only then did they allow a sigh of relief.

That relief was short-lived because as C.J. reached for the brass handle of the old oak front door, it flew open and they were confronted by a woman who was not too happy with them.

Edna MacGregor seemed to fill the doorway as she demanded to know where they had been.

C.J. opened his mouth to answer her. She didn't wait for him to speak.

"When we said you could walk home and enjoy the cool evening," she said, "we didn't say that you could stay out until all hours of the night."

"They were only gone for less than an hour," Jackson said.

Jackson's statement didn't faze her. "You get in here and explain yourselves," she said.

She backed up and allowed them to enter the house. The five kids filed in and entered the front parlor, which was the only room with a light on. Edna and Jackson followed them in. Everyone else, including old Mrs. Wesley, was waiting for them.

There were no places for them to sit, as every available seat was in use by the adults. Even Mrs. Wesley's rocking chair was in the corner to make room for everyone.

They stood in the center of the room, surrounded by unhappy faces.

The room was quiet for several minutes. They knew they had to tell their parents something about what had happened. C.J. wasn't sure how much to tell.

Angus cleared his throat and started the questioning with a simple statement. "You didn't come directly back," he said.

"I didn't know what happened to you," Edna said. "Someone could have kidnapped you for all we knew."

She wasn't far off the mark. C.J. remained silent.

"I was at my wit's end," Edna continued, and then stopped when a soft voice from the corner rocker interrupted her.

"Let them tell their story," Mrs. Wesley said and then rocked quietly again while she worked on her cross-stitching and listened.

Everyone quieted down for the explanation.

The time had come to tell them exactly what had happened, and since C.J. suggested they walked back to the house, he started the tale.

"I wanted to talk with them about something," he said, pointing at the other four Young Explorers. "So I suggested walking, and we ended up walking slower than we realized."

"It still wouldn't take you more than one hour to get back," Angus said.

"What was so important?" Edna asked.

Sadie tried not to get sidetracked. She ignored the question and continued C.J.'s story. "Before we got to the end of Elm Street," she said, "we heard someone following us."

Several of the adults took a sharp breath, but everyone remained silent this time and waited for them to continue.

"We couldn't outrun him to the house," Scotty picked up the story. "So I ran ahead to find a place to hide. I found that the side door to the blacksmith's shop was unlocked. We hid in there."

"Breaking and entering?" Walter asked.

"Actually," Frederick said, "we only entered. We didn't have time to worry about it then. We barely had time to hide before someone followed us in."

Laura then launched into telling them about the demand to return the ticket to the museum and the threat to them if they didn't.

Then the flood of questions began.

"Did you recognize the man?" Angus asked.

Frederick shook his head. "It was too dark," he said. "I wasn't even sure it was a man at first."

"How about his voice?" Walter asked. "Could you recognize his voice if you heard it again?"

"No," Sadie said, taking charge of the question. "It was a gruff whisper." She thought for a moment. "I think it was a man too, but I don't know who."

"Why did someone want you to return the ticket?" Angus asked. "Wasn't it already at the museum?"

All eyes went to C.J.

"I took the ticket from the museum," he said and produced the ticket from his pocket.

Angus held out his hand, and C.J. handed it to him. After checking it to see that it was the ticket they had found in the river bottom and making sure he hadn't damaged it further, he set it down on a table next to him. He nodded to C.J. to continue.

"Mayor Danford and Mr. Penn seemed overly interested in the ticket," C.J. said. "It was as if they were having a tug of war over it. I took it to keep it safe."

It was then that the old woman spoke again. She had put down her needlework and was standing, though no one heard her rise.

"The ticket is safe," she said, "and these young boys and girls are safe. I think it's time for all of us to get some rest."

After some quick glances around the room, smiles broke out on each face. The adults couldn't believe what was happening. Someone who was old enough to be their mother was shooing them off to bed.

"You're right, Mrs. Wesley," Angus said. "We are all happy that they are back safe and sound. We can deal with the rest in the morning." He turned to the kids. "From now on, try to stay out of trouble."

They each said good night and headed to bed.

For a time, there was soft talking among people sharing rooms as they prepared for bed and the sound of bedsprings as they finally retired for the night.

They extinguished the lights and exchanged last minute good night wishes. Then everyone settled down and drifted off to sleep.

The house was dark and quiet, and for a time, all occupants were where they should be for the rest of the night.

Then, there was movement in the third-floor hallway as first one shadowy figure and then another crept out of their rooms. They paused in the hallway and listened for any sounds from the other bedrooms. Then they moved to the door of the room where C.J. and Scotty slept.

A third figure appeared and joined them at the door. They tapped softly. A moment later, the door opened, and they rushed into the room. A match flared, a candle was lit, and the five Young Explorers stood facing each other.

"I couldn't sleep," Sadie said and plopped down on the end of C.J.'s bed. "I can't seem to get that ticket out of my mind."

"That's bothering me too," Frederick said. He sat on the floor and leaned back against Scotty's bed.

"I'm more worried about the person following us," Laura said. She took one look at Scotty sitting on his bed and sat down next to Sadie. "Even if we return the ticket, I'm not sure he'll leave us alone."

"I can't sleep either," Scotty said as he looked around at everyone, "because of all the people in my room." Everyone ignored his comment.

"Why would anyone want that ticket?" Sadie asked. "It's been sitting at the bottom of the river for almost thirty years. We're lucky that we found it and it's in one piece."

C.J. sat down on his bed and slid back until he sat with his back to the wall. "It doesn't have any value. I mean, it's not like it's money or anything."

"It's a train ticket," Frederick said. "We don't even know who it belongs to except that it was a girl."

"A woman," Sadie said.

Frederick rolled his eyes. "A woman or a girl, that purse could have belonged to either," he said.

"It isn't good for anything," C.J. said. "It's not evidence that anyone could use to figure out who Junior is."

Laura leaned back against the wall and turned to C.J. "Why would that matter?" She asked.

"Why else would the mayor and Mr. Penn be after it?" C.J. asked. "The only reason they could be interested in the ticket is if it could prove that the mayor is Junior."

"Do you think it was one of them that threatened us?" Scotty asked.

"I don't know," C.J. said. "It's hard to know who wants it if we don't know why they want it."

"It's a train ticket and an old one at that," Sadie said. She got up and went to the window. She looked out into the darkness of the night toward the point where the train had crashed so many years before. "It was only good for getting on a train."

"It's not good for that anymore," Scotty said. "That train is gone."

C.J. snapped his fingers. "It wasn't for just any train," he said. "It was for the Phantom Express."

"We know that," Frederick said. "Tell us something we don't know."

C.J. scooted off his bed. "Remember when Laura tried to get on the train?" he asked.

"I don't," Laura said.

Sadie turned from the window. "What about it?"

"The conductor asked if she had a ticket," C.J. said.

Scotty lay back in his bed. "So what?" he asked.

Sadie brightened. "He sounded like he wanted her to have a ticket." She looked around at Laura, Scotty, and Frederick, who looked back at her with puzzled looks. "He's looking for someone with a ticket."

"Why?" Frederick asked.

"Because," C.J. said, "they're still waiting for one more passenger. They're waiting for Junior to board and warn them of the danger."

Chapter 11

C.J. woke to the smell of breakfast wafting up from the kitchen two floors below his room. He breathed in the delicious smells of bacon and warm maple syrup. He hopped out of bed and nudged Scotty, who was snoring away.

By the time the Young Explorers had returned to their bedrooms, there was precious little time left for sleep. C.J. was fine with a bit of sleep. But Scotty needed his, or he'd be a bear all day. That day, he'd be a bear.

They quickly dressed and, on the way down, met up with the others, who were also in various states of sleep deprivation.

When they reached the main floor, C.J. noticed the flowered suitcases in the front entry that he'd seen before. He glanced into the parlor on his way to the dining room, and there sat Mrs. Wesley in the dim light of the morning with the drapes drawn, rocking in her chair. She was busy with her needlework.

"Good morning, Mrs. Wesley," he said.

She looked up and smiled at him. "Good morning," she said. "Were you up late last night?"

The question startled C.J. "A bit, I guess," he said.

She nodded and went back to the cross-stitching.

"Are you going somewhere?" C.J. asked.

"Going somewhere?" She asked, looking up at him again. "I haven't gone anywhere for a very long time."

"Aren't those your bags in the entryway," he asked, "with red and white flowers on them?"

She nodded again and fished out another color of cross-stitch floss from a basket beside her chair. "That sounds like my luggage," she said.

"They look like they're packed and ready to go in the entryway," C.J. said.

The old woman smiled and shook her head. "I'm not going anywhere," she said and worked on her project again.

C.J. was about to leave her to her needlework when he stopped. "Mrs. Wesley," he said, "do you know why anyone would want a ticket for the Express?"

She suddenly put down her needlework and leaned forward in the rocker. "That is an important ticket," she said in a hushed voice. "You need to protect it."

C.J. hurried over to the old woman and sat on a stool next to her. "That's what we thought," he said.

She leaned back and began rocking again. She closed her eyes and looked as if she had fallen asleep.

"I think the Phantom Express is waiting for someone to use that ticket," he told her. He waited for a reply. She slowly rocked in the chair. "Someone needs to get on the train and stop it," he said.

The woman's eyes remained closed. She smiled. "I knew you were a bright boy," she said softly.

"Breakfast is ready," Angus called out.

The smell of the bacon, eggs, and pancakes with maple syrup made everyone hungry. No one needed another invitation. Soon, everyone gathered around the table and admired the plates piled high with their delicious breakfast.

As he sat down, Angus noticed everyone was there except one. "Where is Mrs. Wesley?" he asked.

"She's in the front parlor," C.J. said. "I'll get her."

When he went into the front parlor, Mrs. Wesley wasn't there. The rocker sat empty, and the needlework the woman had been working on was gone.

C.J. joined them at the breakfast table again. "She wasn't there," he said.

"Maybe she isn't hungry," Edna said. "I haven't seen her eat much at all since we've been here."

Soon they forgot Mrs. Wesley. The diners were busy helping themselves to the tasty dishes Walter and Edna had whipped up that morning.

The pace of eating slowed until every one of them had pushed back from the table and declared that they were stuffed. Little remained of the food since no one wanted to waste even a morsel.

"Dad, what are you going to do with the ticket?" C.J. asked when he was done.

"Some of us talked about that this morning while making breakfast," Angus said as he wiped his mouth with his napkin. "We decided that we're going down to the sheriff's office and report last night's incident."

"Who's we?" C.J. asked. He was sure that he knew the answer already.

"That would be me and the five of you," he said to the Young Explorers. "You're all witnesses."

"What about the ticket?" C.J. asked again. "What will happen to that?"

"They will probably consider it evidence," Angus said. "The sheriff will hold on to it."

"Will he return it to the museum?" C.J. asked.

"I don't know," Angus told him. "That would be up to the sheriff."

"If he returns it, somebody might steal it," C.J. said.

"It's not our concern," Angus said. "We leave that decision to the sheriff."

C.J. looked across the table at the faces of Sadie, Scotty, Laura, and Frederick. They all thought the same as he did.

He closed his eyes and breathed deeply to clear his brain so he could think. After a few minutes, his eyes flew open, and he said, "I have an idea."

As the sun set, C.J. started down the street from the old Victorian mansion headed toward the museum. He walked alone down the middle of the street and held the ticket in front of him, clearly visible to anyone who wanted to see it.

There were still a few people on the street. Except for a glance or two at the boy, no one took notice of him and no one paid any attention to the ticket.

He kept an eye out for either of his two suspects, the current mayor of Danford, Jefferson Danford, Jr., or his opponent in the election, Henry Penn. He saw neither one during his short walk.

He stopped at the door of the museum and held the ticket so that anyone watching would know that he had it. After a pause, he opened the door and went in.

The curator was the only person in the museum's lobby. He nodded to the boy as he came in, but didn't speak with him. He simply opened the door into the museum's main display room and allowed C.J. to enter.

C.J. went to the display case where the ticket had been the night before. The curator had packed up and put away all the other artifacts. He placed the ticket on the glass at the center of the display case and looked around. There were two windows that opened into the room, but it was too dark to see if anyone was watching him.

He glanced up at the sliver of the moon that shone through the skylight and exited the room with the curator. Both of them crossed to the outside door and went through it back out onto the street. C.J. waited as the curator locked the door and pocketed the key.

Without a word, they looked at each other and then turned and went their separate ways down the street. The curator headed home, and C.J. walked back toward the mansion where they stayed.

Although the walk wasn't a long one, two city blocks, it seemed a long one to C.J. He felt eyes on him the entire way as he walked along

Elm Street until he reached the corner. He didn't know if it was his imagination or whether someone actually watched him.

When he reached the corner, he glanced back over his shoulder. Although it was almost dark, there was still plenty of light to see anyone who was on the street. There was no one. He took a deep breath and turned the corner.

Inside the museum, Angus sat in the darkness of the curator's office. Except for the soft breathing of the sheriff and the Young Explorers who sat around the cramped space with him, the building was silent.

Angus hadn't wanted the kids to be at the museum, but they had insisted, and the sheriff himself had come into the argument on their side.

"They will be easier to guard at the museum," the sheriff had said. "That way, I don't have to split up my men to guard two places."

Angus hoped he was right.

"The boy has done his part," the sheriff whispered. "Now we wait and see if our visitor shows up."

Angus sat in the dark with his eyes closed, listening for any sound that would show that their quarry was at hand. When C.J. had explained his plan at breakfast, it seemed relatively safe. There in the dark, the danger seemed more real.

"Your men are in place?" he asked in a whisper.

"We went over this already," the sheriff said in a voice barely audible to Angus. He realized that the man wanted to be reassured, so he repeated the setup. "Two deputies are inside the building watching the windows and doors," he said. "Two others are watching from the outside."

Angus had closed his eyes again when there was the sound of a board creaking somewhere out in the museum lobby. His eyes flew open, and he sat bolt upright. He still couldn't see anything in the windowless office, and his ears strained to hear any noise.

Another board creaked outside the door of the office. Both he and the sheriff slowly rose to their feet and turned to where they knew the door was.

There was a click of the latch as the knob turned and the door slowly swung inward.

"Sheriff," a low voice whispered into the room. It was a deputy. "The boy's here," he said.

Angus heard the soft step of his son as he entered the room. "This way," Angus said. "Follow my voice."

C.J. made his way across the room to his father and sat down on the floor next to his chair. He felt his father's hand squeeze his shoulder.

After he returned to the house, he ducked out the back door and made his way the long way around to the tracks and followed them back to the museum. The deputy at the back door waited for him and delivered him to the curator's office.

His father guided him over to where the other Young Explorers sat on the floor and waited.

There was excited chattering among the five until Angus shushed them. "You need to be quiet," he told them in a whisper.

Angus and the sheriff settled back into their chairs, and they began their quiet vigil again.

Time ticked away. The kids got restless, but they understood the importance of being quiet and made little noise. Angus almost fell asleep once and jerked awake again and the adrenaline rush kept him awake for a long time afterward.

At one point, everyone in the room was scared half to death when Scotty suddenly sneezed. After a little laughter at the fright, they settled down into silence once again.

Now and again, a deputy would approach the office door, quietly open it and report to the sheriff that there was still no sign of anyone approaching the building.

Then, late into the night, they heard the tinkling sound of glass breaking somewhere in the museum.

Angus and the sheriff were on their feet at once. They carefully moved to the door, and the sheriff eased it open. In the light from the front window, they saw a deputy pointing to the door into the museum's main display room, showing that the sound came from there.

"Stay here," Angus whispered to the kids and went out into the lobby with the sheriff.

The kids were immediately on their feet and making their way to the door. By the time they entered the museum lobby, the sheriff, his deputy, and Angus slipped through the door into the main room.

They hurried across the room to the door and peered through to see what was happening.

High above the floor of the museum, the broken skylight window lifted, and C.J. felt a cool breeze blow into the room. He pointed up to it in case one of the other Young Explorers hadn't noticed it yet.

After the window of the skylight had disappeared, a rope dropped and hung from the roof.

Everyone waited, and for a long time, nothing else happened. Then, a pair of legs dangled down, and soon someone slowly climbed down the rope. When the figure reached the floor, it moved over to the display case where the ticket waited.

"Halt," the sheriff yelled. "You are under arrest."

The two deputies pulled the covers off of their lanterns, and the room flooded with light. In the center of the room by the display, a person held an arm up to block the blinding light and dashed back to the rope.

As the sheriff and his deputies closed in, he saw retreat up the rope would be impossible.

They wrestled with the intruder, but the figure escaped and dashed to the door where the kids stood.

As the figure came to a stop in front of them, they saw by the light of the lanterns that it was Henry Penn.

Chapter 12

"Henry Penn?" the sheriff said. It was all he seemed to think of saying when he saw the man standing before him.

Henry ran back toward the rope still hanging from the ceiling. He tried to leap over the display case and grab the ticket but missed.

Broken glass and artifacts scattered everywhere as the case shattered and Henry sprawled onto the floor. He was back up on his feet in a moment.

"Henry," the sheriff said, "you are under arrest for attempted robbery and threatening those kids."

Henry just laughed and began backing away from the sheriff and his deputies.

"This is not a laughing matter," the sheriff said. He signaled for the two deputies to flank the man.

"That's nothing," Henry said, still chuckling. He kept his eyes mostly on Angus and the sheriff, who faced him down, but his eyes also darted to the sides where the deputies edged around him. "I'm wanted for far more than that."

"What do you mean?" the sheriff asked.

"I'm a mass murderer," he said with a laugh. "Didn't you know that?"

"Mass murderer?" the sheriff repeated.

"I've killed over 100 men, women and children," he said.

The sheriff looked at him blankly.

"He's Junior," C.J. said. "That's why he didn't want me to talk about it. It wasn't the mayor. It was him."

"Smart boy," Henry said. "My real name is Henry Penny, Jr. I'm Jake Penny's brother."

"So Junior was here all along," the sheriff said.

"My parents dropped the Y from our last name when Jake started his gang," Henry said. "They wanted to protect themselves and me."

"You joined his gang anyway," Angus said.

"Jake tried to get me to join. The train was supposed to be my first job," he said. "I chickened out."

"If you didn't help your brother," the sheriff said, "you are innocent."

"Innocent?" he said. "I wasn't on that train to stop it. All of those people died because of me."

The sheriff gave a slight nod to his deputies, and they closed in on the man. The sheriff blew a whistle to call the other deputies in from outside.

Henry was ready for them. He dropped back and rolled under one of the display cases. Back on his feet, he ran for the rear door of the museum.

Before he could get there, one deputy burst through the door. Changing his direction slightly, he ran straight to the back window and launched himself through it. The glass shattered into dozens of deadly shards, and he was gone.

Amid the chaos, Laura picked through the remains of the display case and reached down to pick up the gold watch. She held it up and gazed at it as the lantern light reflected into her eyes.

"He's not here," the deputy said after searching the area behind the museum.

"Fan out and search the streets," the sheriff told him. "Send someone to his house. Find him."

After the deputies had gone, the sheriff turned to Angus. "We should take the kids back to the Rose," he said. "With Penn...Penny," he corrected himself, "out there somewhere, they may be targets."

Angus agreed with him and called to his son, "C.J., we all better get back to the house. I don't want you kids out while that man is on the loose."

C.J. looked around. "Where's Sadie?"

Sadie popped up from behind the shattered display case with an armload of museum pieces. "I'm here," she said. "Picking up some of this stuff."

"Don't worry about that," Angus told her. "Stack it over there and let's go. Where's your brother?"

"I'm here too," Scotty said, standing up next to his sister with more artifacts.

"Where's Laura?" Frederick asked.

They glanced around the room. There was no sign of Laura. A further search showed she was not there.

"You all stay in this room," Angus said. "I'll check in the office to see if she went back in there."

Angus checked the lobby and the front door. The locked door showed Laura could not have gone that direction, so he went into the office. He flipped on the lights and squinted at the sudden brightness. There was no sign of her.

When he returned to the main room, they all looked up at him expectantly. He shook his head.

"Where would she have gone?" Angus asked. No one had an answer for him.

C.J. rushed over to the museum pieces that Sadie and Scotty had picked up and scattered them across the table.

Angus frowned at his son. "What are you doing?"

C.J. didn't answer. He scanned the scattered mess.

"What are you looking for?" Sadie asked.

"The ticket," C.J. said. "I'm looking for the ticket." He kicked a pile of debris and moved on to another.

The others joined in. Soon it was apparent that the ticket was not there.

A deputy returned from the search. He stood for a moment and watched everyone digging through the mess. Then he got the attention of the sheriff by clearing his throat.

"There's no sign of the suspect," he said. "We checked his house. The housekeeper said he hadn't been there since before the debate. Anderson is watching it now."

"Keep searching," the sheriff said.

The deputy had just disappeared out the door again when the sheriff yelled for him to come back. He poked his bald head through the doorway.

"A girl has gone missing," the sheriff told him. He gave the deputy a quick description of Laura. "Keep an eye out for her."

"Will do," the deputy said and disappeared again.

"The ticket isn't here," Sadie said.

"Help me," C.J. said, pointing to the other end of the display table.

Together they tried to lift it up but couldn't. Frederick and Scotty joined in, and soon they had it righted and in place. After scanning the area where it had fallen, C.J. said, "We've lost it."

"Did Mr. Penny pick it up?" Sadie asked Angus and the sheriff. "Did anyone see him take it?"

The sheriff shook his head. "I didn't see him pick it up, and I don't think he had time."

"We watched him the whole time," Angus added, "at least until he crashed through that window."

"Who else would have taken it?" Scotty asked.

"Look for the watch," C.J. suddenly said. He sifted through the debris once again.

"What watch?" the sheriff asked.

"It's a gold pocket watch," Angus said. "It belonged to the conductor of the Express. They found it hanging off the old trestle."

"What does that have to do with the ticket?"

Angus had to admit that he was as confused as the sheriff. "I don't know," he said.

"It's not here," C.J. said when the search ended. "I think Laura took both the watch and the ticket."

The sheriff stared at C.J. "What does she want with a pocket watch and a ticket for a train that crashed thirty years ago?" he asked.

"That's what I wondered," Angus said. "What haven't you been telling us?"

C.J. looked down at some papers piled where Sadie had left them. He ruffled through them absentmindedly while he thought about where to start.

"I don't think she wanted the watch," he said. "I think the watch wanted her."

Everyone looked at him in confusion.

"I mean," he continued, "the night we found the watch, Laura took it. Or it took her, and she tried to board the Phantom Express."

"And you didn't tell us?" Angus asked.

C.J. avoided his gaze and continued his explanation. "She couldn't board because she didn't have a ticket."

"Even if I believed you," the sheriff said, "about a ghost train and all, why would she want to board it?"

"To stop it," C.J. said. "To warn the conductor to stop the train and prevent it from crashing."

"You're saying that it keeps coming back and crashing because it's waiting for Junior to board it and break the cycle?" Angus asked.

"Well, not Junior necessarily," C.J. said. "Someone who has a ticket, the ticket that Junior should have used that night."

"Someone like Laura," Sadie said, interrupting them. "Someone lured by the power of the watch to use the ticket."

"If you ask anyone around here, they will tell you that the Phantom Express is just a legend," the sheriff said. He went to the broken window at the back of the museum and gazed out at the tracks in the darkness.

"No one admits they believe in it. The only time anyone will talk about it is when some kid tells the story to scare his little sister."

"It's not a legend," Sadie said. "It's true."

The sheriff turned back to them. "You're telling me you believe in ghosts?" he asked.

"I do," Frederick said.

"So do I," Scotty chimed in.

"Add me to that list," Sadie said.

"We all do," C.J. said. "Don't we, Dad?"

"You believe this malarkey?" the sheriff asked.

"After what we saw in Peru," Angus said. "I have to admit that I can't rule it out."

"We saw it at the station the other night," C.J. said, going to the window and pointing out at the tracks. "It was right there, as big as day, and lit up like a Christmas tree."

Sadie picked up the story. "The conductor, the one in that picture," she said and stabbed a finger at the man in the picture on the wall, "stepped off the train and asked us if we had a ticket."

"He asked Laura if she had a ticket," Scotty corrected her. "I think he sensed she had his watch."

"And later, after it pulled out of the station," Frederick said, "we heard it crash off the bridge."

"You really expect me to believe a bunch of kids saw a ghost train?" the sheriff asked.

Angus looked at the four Young Explorers and thought back to their adventure with the wraith in Peru. "Yes," he said after a moment, "you should believe them."

"You too?" the sheriff said. "A man of your reputation believes in ghosts?"

Before Angus could respond, the sorrowful sound of a train whistle echoed through the town and the slow chugging of a steam train rolling to a stop floated in through the open window.

They hurried to the window and door and looked out at a train approaching the station.

"The Phantom Express," C.J. said. "It's here."

The sheriff rushed out to the narrow space behind the museum. He saw the train pulling into the station over the fence between the two buildings.

The only ways around the fence were to step out onto the tracks in front of the moving train or go out the street side. The sheriff chose the street.

Angus and the kids rushed behind the sheriff, trying to keep up with him.

By the time they rounded the fence and made their way around to the platform, they heard the release of steam from the engine and the whistle that meant the train was in the station.

C.J. turned to the sheriff. "Do you believe us now?" he asked the man.

The sheriff nodded his head slowly.

There it was. The Phantom Express was at the station, lit up by a ghostly light. As C.J. had said, it was lit up like a Christmas tree. He looked from car to car. Each had the Dakota and Western Express name across the top.

"We knew it was real," the sheriff said. "But we would never admit it, especially to outsiders."

As they stood there staring, the shadowy figures of station attendants appeared from nowhere and filled the engine with water from the tank towering over it.

They heard the clack of latches as the doors opened to the cars, and shadowy attendants stepped out to help passengers disembark and embark.

Both Angus and the sheriff gaped at the train.

C.J. tugged at his father's arm. "We have to watch for Laura and Mr. Penny," he told him. "The one who has the ticket will try to board the train."

They both nodded, but the sight of the phantom train still mesmerized them.

One by one, the deputies arrived at the platform and each stopped cold and stared at the train.

C.J. turned to his friends. "Keep an eye out for Laura. I'm sure she has the watch." He glanced around. If she also had the ticket, she'll be in trouble.

The engine let out another cloud of steam that filled the platform and temporarily blocked their view of the attendants waiting at the car doors for travelers who would not be coming that night.

As the steam evaporated and more of the platform came back into view, it horrified them to see Laura approaching a large man standing at the far door.

"That's the conductor," C.J. said and took the steps to the platform three at a time. The others followed.

She held out the ticket to the conductor, and he smiled at her. Before they could cross the platform, he had taken the ticket and punched it for her.

They reached the conductor as she stepped up onto the first of the steps up into the car. They tried to go around him, but he blocked them.

"Sorry," he said. His voice seemed to come from a faraway place. "There is no more room on this train."

They yelled Laura's name. She glanced back at them, smiled and climbed to the platform at the back of the car. A moment later, she disappeared into the ghostly light of the Phantom Express.

Chapter 13

"We have to get on board," C.J. said, trying to push past the conductor.

He was much bigger than C.J. and very strong. He grabbed C.J.'s collar and hauled him back. "No one is going on board the train," he said.

Frederick tried next, with the same result. To surprise the man, he tried a wrestling move to trip him and land him flat on his back, but he ended up almost falling himself.

The conductor shoved the two boys back and stood with a hand on a pistol that hung on his belt. "I don't like to use this," he said, "but I will if I'm forced to." He glared at them sternly. "Don't force me to."

C.J. tried a different tack. "Mr. Olson, we don't want to take the train," he said. "We just want to get our friend who shouldn't be on it."

"Does your friend have a ticket?" the conductor asked. "No one can board without a ticket."

"She had a ticket," Sadie said. "But the ticket wasn't hers. It belonged to someone else."

"Did she steal it?" the man asked. His hand went to the pistol again.

"No," C.J. said, "she shouldn't have used it. She doesn't belong on this train."

"She needs to stay here with us," Sadie said, "not go with you on the train."

"We've been waiting a long time for our last passenger," the conductor told her, "a very long time. And now that passenger is on board."

"She's not the right passenger," Frederick said. "You're looking for Junior and he hasn't arrived yet."

"We have all the passengers we need," the conductor told him. "We are full, and as soon as they finish filling the boiler, this train leaves. You should all head on home now. It's late."

The four Young Explorers huddled together to figure out what to do next.

"I don't think we can get by the conductor or any of the other attendants," Sadie said. She looked at the other men on the platform. One had bright red hair, one had white hair and the last one was blond. "They think they've found their lost passenger and don't want anyone else on board."

"Can we stop it from leaving?" Scotty asked.

"It's a ghost train," Frederick said. "It shouldn't be here at all. What can we do to keep it here?"

"Maybe there's another way on board," C.J. said.

There was a commotion beside the platform as the Halls, the MacGregors and Axel Van Housen arrived, snapping the other adults out of their fascination with the Phantom Express.

"Where is Laura?" Teresa asked.

"I think she's on the train," the bald deputy said.

The Halls climbed to the platform and rushed across to the conductor. The rest of the group followed. The sheriff and his deputies came up behind them. They all pushed between the Young Explorers and the conductor.

"Where is my daughter?" Teresa demanded, stepping right up to the man. "Is she on the train?"

The sheriff pushed through the crowd and pulled Teresa back from the conductor. "You are the conductor on this train?" he asked the man.

"I am," the conductor said.

"I am looking for a missing girl, and I believe she is on this train," the sheriff said. "My men and I need to search the train and find her."

"I'm sorry," the conductor said, "that is impossible. This is a special line. No one can board without a ticket." He glanced at the sheriff and each of his deputies. "Do any of you have a ticket?"

"I don't need a ticket," the sheriff said, his voice rising in anger. He grabbed at the badge on his shirt. "This is the only ticket I need to get on this train."

"You have no power on board this train," the conductor told him coldly.

"Please," Teresa said, clasping her hands in front of her. "My daughter is on this train. She's not one of you. She shouldn't be in there."

"I'm sorry, Ma'am," the conductor said softly. "She had a ticket." He raised his voice so that everyone could hear. "Now, the train is preparing to leave. Please step away from the edge of the platform."

Teresa turned to the sheriff. "You can't let them take Laura," she said. "Do something."

The sheriff waved his deputies in closer. "It looks like we'll need to force our way onto this train. You can use your guns, but only if it is necessary."

"Isn't this supposed to be a ghost train?" one deputy asked. "Will guns work on them?"

"I don't know. We have to try something," the sheriff said. He turned to Angus. "You and your group take the kids and leave the area. We don't want you to get hurt."

"Where are the kids?" Walter asked.

They looked all around the platform. There was no sign of them. The kids were gone.

"Damn it," the sheriff said. "We'll have to look for them when we're done here. Right now, you all have to leave the area. We don't want any of you hurt if there is gunfire."

Teresa wanted to say something more. She stepped toward the conductor, then allowed herself to be led away by her husband and the other parents.

Once they were gone, the sheriff turned to the conductor, who was watching for a sign from the engineer that they were ready to leave. "Did you let the other children on board?" the sheriff asked.

"No," the conductor told him. "Only passengers with tickets embarked, and no passengers disembarked."

They allowed the conductor to go back to work and as soon as he was not paying any attention to them, the sheriff nodded his head and shouted, "Now!"

The seven men drew their weapons. Some rushed the conductor, while others ran to the train doors.

When the men tried to get their hands on the conductor, he simply vanished, leaving them grabbing at air and looking confused.

The men rushing the train stopped in their tracks when the doors began slamming shut one by one until the train was closed up and the platform was left dark and deserted.

They tried the doors. They found them locked. One deputy tried to shoot the door, but the bullets didn't affect the train at all.

"Stop shooting," the sheriff said.

As soon as the shooting stopped, the Halls ran back onto the platform. Teresa stopped in her tracks when she saw the train was closed up and ready to leave.

"What happened?" Jackson asked. "You weren't able to get on the train?"

"No," the sheriff said. He told them what had happened when they had rushed the conductor.

Teresa broke down. The sheriff and Jackson led her to a bench. Edna sat with Teresa to comfort her.

The sheriff went to his deputies and spoke to them in a low voice. When they finished talking, the deputies left the platform. When he returned to the others, the sheriff said, "I sent them to look for the kids."

"Isn't there anything we can do?" Jackson said. "You know she's on board. Can't you get her out?"

"I wish I could," the sheriff said. "I'm out of ideas." He scanned their faces and saw shock and disappointment. The disappointment was with him. "If anyone has any ideas on how to get a little girl off a ghost train that by all rights should not even exist, I am open to suggestions."

They looked at each other. None of them had any other suggestions.

The sheriff looked at the train. "We can only hope that she can give the warning and end the cycle."

Some time before all the commotion on the platform, C.J. and the other Young Explorers sneaked off and hid in the heavy underbrush that grew on the other side of the tracks in the train's shadow.

They decided it was time to put their hastily prepared plan in motion before the train started moving. C.J. jumped from the bushes and the rest followed him.

They hurried to the last train car, an observation car where there was a balcony facing the tracks behind the train. C.J. stepped gingerly onto the first step, and when nothing happened, climbed up to the platform. The others quickly followed him.

They huddled down at the rear door below the window that looked into the train. C.J. raised himself up far enough to glimpse the inside of the car through the window.

"It looks deserted," he whispered to the others.

He dropped again and reached for the handle of the door. This was the moment of truth. Their plans all hinged on being able to get on board, and that meant they had to get through that door.

He pulled the handle down and with a clunk, the door unlatched. They all tensed at the loud sound.

C.J. rose again to look through the window. "Still empty," he whispered after he had dropped back down again.

They all breathed a sigh of relief. There was at least some luck on their side.

C.J. opened the door, trying not to make any noise.

Once the door was open far enough that they could squeeze in, C.J. slipped inside. He checked the passage again and then waved in the next one in line.

Sadie slipped in next to C.J. He told her to keep watch while he let in Scotty and Frederick.

Once they were all in, C.J. quietly shut the door again and then put his finger to his lips.

They rushed up the aisle to the other end of the car. They opened the door, hopped from one car to the platform of the next, and ducked down again.

They could hear their parents and the sheriff arguing with the conductor. Luckily for them, the observation car was not alongside the platform. The adults couldn't see them between the cars.

C.J. stood to look through the window. "It's a sleeper car," he whispered after dropping back down.

The attendants made the beds up, and each had curtains hanging across, giving the bunk a small amount of privacy. A narrow passage led through the car.

"The attendant is gone," he whispered.

C.J. pushed the door open and slipped inside. The others followed in behind.

They all listened for anyone in the car, but there were no sounds in the passageway at all.

"So far, so good," C.J. whispered to the others.

C.J. turned to Scotty. "OK, we're on board," he said. "What do we have to do to stop this train?"

"There are two ways," Scotty told them. "The first way will be tough. We can try to persuade the conductor to signal the engineer to stop."

"He didn't seem like he wanted to cooperate with us," Sadie said.

"Not at all," C.J. agreed. "We can probably scratch that one. What's the other way?"

"It has its drawbacks too," Scotty said. "We can try to persuade the engineer to stop the train."

"That means we have to go through the entire train," Frederick said.

"Exactly," Scotty said.

"So," C.J. said. "You're saying we have to sneak through half a dozen train cars and avoid the conductor so he doesn't throw us off the train?"

"Definitely avoid the conductor," Scotty agreed.

"And the other attendants," Sadie added.

"And the other attendants," C.J. said. "Climb around the engine without falling off. Convince the engineer and fireman that we are not train robbers and just want them to stop the train before it hits a ghostly pile of logs so that we are not all killed, along with a hundred ghosts that died thirty years ago."

"Exactly," Scotty said.

"We'd hate to do something easy," Frederick said.

"We'd better get moving then," C.J. said.

They stood up and made their way through the sleeper car to the door at the other end.

They were almost halfway through the car when they heard shouts and doors slamming. Then there was the sound of gunfire.

They all dropped to the floor of the car and covered their heads. When the gunfire stopped, they looked around at each other. It surprised them that with all the bullets flying around, none hit them.

The whistle sounded and echoed across the town.

"The train is about to leave the station," Scotty told them. "We have to hurry."

They jumped to their feet and headed to the front of the sleeper. They hadn't gone far when the car jolted as the train pulled out of the station. It knocked them off their feet again.

After they recovered, C.J. told them, "It only takes ten or fifteen minutes to get to the bridge. We need to stop this train. Now!"

Chapter 14

The Young Explorers ran to the far end of the car.

They were almost there when a hand reached out from one bunk and caught Frederick's arm, jerking him to a stop.

A wrinkled face poked out from between the curtains. His thin white hair stuck up in every direction.

"What are you doing here?" he asked. "I don't remember seeing you around before."

Frederick pried the cold, gnarled hand off of his arm and backed out of his reach as the old man tried to grab him again.

"We're new," Frederick said as they continued on down the passage.

As they reached the end of the car, they heard something bang on the floor behind them.

C.J. paused before opening the door at the end to look back down the passage.

Nothing had changed as far as he saw. He had expected the old man had jumped from his bunk and was giving chase. But the passage was empty, and the curtains were still drawn across the old man's bunk.

Then he saw the far door's handle twist, and when he heard the latch click open, he didn't waste any time.

"Run," he whispered to the others.

C.J. grabbed the handle to the door at the end of the passage and tugged on it. With some effort, he pulled it open, revealing the open space between that car and the next car in line.

The train was outside of town and the space between the cars was dark despite the glow coming from inside. The cold wind blowing through the space and the clacking sound of the wheels on the track below them told of the danger of falling from the train.

C.J. was the first to cross from the sleeper car to the platform of the next car. The others followed him and soon they were safely inside again.

They found themselves in another sleeper car, an exact duplicate of the one they were just in.

Wasting no time, they rushed down the passage, making sure that they were as close to the center as possible. They watched for grasping hands from the bunks on either side.

Before they reached the end of the car, they heard the door behind swing open and the sound of the wind howling between the cars.

They glanced back. Standing in the doorway was Henry Penny, the younger brother of Jake Penny of the Penny Ante Gang. Junior had found them.

C.J. paid too much attention to the man at the other end of the car as they hurried to the door at the end. He ran so fast that he ran into it hard.

With only a slight pause, he pulled it open and jumped across to the next car and pushed open that door as well.

The rest of the Young Explorers knew Junior was behind them, so they didn't consider the danger on either side of them and leapt across the gap into the next car.

C.J. pushed the door shut and turned to run through the car, but he stopped, with the others colliding to a stop behind him.

They were in a coach car and sitting in every seat was a ghostly passenger. And they were all staring at the kids.

Sadie pulled on C.J.'s arm. "We have to keep moving," she whispered.

They started slowly up the aisle between the seats. C.J. tried to smile at the passengers as they went. He heard Laura and Scotty say hello to some of them. The passengers simply stared at them as they passed.

They picked up their pace and jogged to the other end of the car.

C.J. had just thought that they would make it through when a man wearing an old-fashioned brown suit and tie stood up and blocked their way.

"You don't belong here," he said, pointing at them.

"They're not one of us," a woman said.

"Do they have tickets?" a little girl asked.

"Get the conductor," another man yelled.

C.J. held up his hands to calm them down. "We're here to help," he said.

"Throw them from the train," a boy said. He looked like he might have been a teenager. "They don't belong here."

"We're trying to stop the train," Sadie said, trying to be heard above the din. "We're trying to save you."

C.J. tried to push his way past the man in the suit. The man was strong for a ghost and held him back.

"Grab 'em," a man said. "Don't let 'em get away."

The man grabbed C.J. and flipped him around. C.J. quickly found himself facing his friends with one arm immobilized behind his back and the man's arm around his neck.

Two women each grabbed Sadie by an arm and cackled as they stretched her between them.

Frederick attempted to fight his would-be captor. He soon realized that his blows had no effect on the spirits and gave up.

Scotty tried to get away by crawling under a seat. As he stood up, a swift kick to his shin sent him back to the ground and three rotund children piled on top of him, pinning his arms and legs.

"Stop," a familiar woman's voice cried out. "Let them go."

Henry couldn't believe the kids were on the train. Now, he'd have to deal with them, too.

By the time Henry reached the door leading to the next car, he'd had enough of that ghost train.

Part way through the car, some little brats had tried to swarm him from one bunk and grab his legs as he ran through the car. They tripped him, and he fell heavily to the floor, knocking his head hard on the wood. He had kicked them off of him and got on his feet before they just as quickly crawled through the curtains back into the bunks.

His head pounded as he made his way to the door at the front of the car.

He opened the door and stepped across the gap between the cars and went through into the next one.

The car was full of people who all sat in their seats staring straight forward.

He moved along the aisle between the seats, mindful of any attempt by anyone to reach out and grab him or prevent him from getting through the car.

He saw there was no sign of the kids, so they must have made it through that car without a problem.

Except for one old woman who looked up at him from her needlework and smiled, everyone ignored him as he passed and kept staring straight ahead.

When he reached the other end of the car, he looked back. Everyone was staring right at him.

"Creepy," he mumbled to himself. He grabbed the door handle and went across the platforms and into the next car.

When he heard Henry shut the door again, C.J. slid out from under the seat where the old woman sat and peered over the seat in front of him to check that the man was truly gone.

He called to the rest of his friends to come out of hiding. "Let's go," he said.

Sadie popped out from under a blanket where she pretended to be asleep.

Scotty had been sharing a seat with another boy, and he handed back to the boy the wide-brimmed hat he'd borrowed.

Frederick had also been hiding under a seat and was soon standing in the aisle with the others.

C.J. turned to the woman who had dropped her needlework in her lap. Mrs. Wesley looked up at him and smiled.

"You knew everything about this train," he said.

"I hoped that you all would find something that could help us," she said, her gaze going from one of the Young Explorers to the next.

"I'm sorry you were on here," C.J. told her.

"It was our fate," Mrs. Wesley said. "You can't do anything about that."

The four of them looked around at all the faces of the passengers, who were watching them intently.

"You have little time," Mrs. Wesley said. "You should be on your way."

They said their goodbyes to the woman and hurried to the front of the car.

They glanced through the window toward the next car. Henry was not waiting for them.

"We'll never see her again," Sadie said. "Will we?"

"Only if we warn them in time," C.J. told her. "If we don't, we'll be seeing her a lot." With that, they opened the door and moved through to the next car.

The next car turned out to be another coach. It wasn't nearly so full of ghostly passengers.

There was no sign of Henry, so they hurried on. There were only two more cars before the engine; the dining car and the baggage car. Both Henry and the conductor were likely in the dining car.

None of the passengers paid any attention to them as they passed. As long as they didn't have to fight with them as they had in the other car, they could make up time.

They were almost at the other end of the car when they heard the door of the next car open.

They fell into the nearest empty seat and slouched down far enough to be hidden and still be able to peer through the seats in front of them and see who it was.

They felt the cold wind of the night blow into the car as the door opened and then shut.

The man entering the car was not Henry or the conductor. It was the attendant with blond hair. As he walked down the aisle, one passenger after another talked to him and asked him questions.

"Are they helping us?" C.J. whispered to Frederick, who sat in the seat in front of him.

"Looks like it," he whispered back.

"We could try to run past," C.J. said.

He barely saw Frederick shake his head. "It didn't work last time."

C.J. watched the attendant slowly moving his way closer. His expression showed that they annoyed him with all the questions.

"Maybe these passengers will help us," C.J. said.

"Do you want to take a chance?" Frederick asked.

C.J. noticed Sadie in the seat across the aisle from him, waving frantically.

When he looked over at her, she pointed toward the window seat next to him.

He turned to find Laura sitting there.

"Laura," he whispered. "We finally found you."

Laura didn't reply. She sat perfectly still, staring at the seat in front of her.

C.J. grabbed her arm and tried to get her attention. She seemed to be in a trance-like state. He looked over at Sadie and shrugged his shoulders. He didn't know what to do. Sadie pointed to her hands.

He looked back at Laura's hands and saw what Sadie tried to tell him. Laura held the pocket watch in one hand and the ticket in the other.

C.J. took hold of the watch chain and tried to pull it out of her hand. Her grip was too tight. He pulled her fingers away from the watch and tugged at the chain. After several tries, it came free, and he held it dangling in the air. He immediately closed his eyes and shoved the watch into his pocket. There was no reason to risk being mesmerized by it himself.

"Where am I?" Laura asked in a voice that was much too loud and made C.J. cringe.

He shushed her and whispered, "We're on the Express and we need to stop it."

"How did we get on?" she asked.

"It's a long story," C.J. told her. "Right now, we have to get to the engine and warn them to stop before we get to the bridge."

"You still want to rush him?" Frederick asked.

C.J. glanced over the seat at the attendant, who was talking to a young boy about the train. "We don't have any other choice," he said.

He signaled their plan to Sadie, and she relayed it to Scotty, who sat in the seat in front of her.

When they all gave him the thumbs up, he turned to Laura. "Are you ready?" he asked.

She nodded her head.

"Now," C.J. yelled, and they jumped out of the seats.

Their plan stopped before it started and it had nothing to do with the attendant.

Just as C.J. leapt out of his seat, someone yanked him backward and shoved him into the seat behind him. The strong hand of Henry Penny gripped his shoulder and held him in the seat.

The man reached down and grabbed the watch chain that hung out of the boy's pocket and pulled it out.

"Thank you," he said and pocketed the watch.

"Now," he said to Laura, who stood in the aisle with the other three kids, "if you would be so kind as to hand over the ticket."

Chapter 15

Sadie stood defiantly in front of Henry Penny. "Let him go," she told him.

He smiled at her. "Gladly," he said. "Hand over the ticket and you can all go on with your lives."

"And if we don't?" Scotty asked.

"This won't end well," Junior said, "for any of us."

Frederick turned, expecting the attendant to be coming for them. The man stood there in the aisle, looking at them. A well-dressed, older man with a cane whispered something to the attendant.

"Let him go," Sadie said. "There's not much time."

"I know," Henry told her. "So hand over the ticket before it's too late."

A commotion toward the front of the car interrupted them. They turned to find the attendant struggling with several of the passengers.

"Let me go," he cried. "They don't belong here."

"Laura," C.J. yelled, "look out."

When the kids turned back, Henry lunged for the ticket in Laura's hand. Before he got a hold of it, Frederick stepped between them and collided with the big man.

They fell in a heap, with Henry on top of Frederick and Laura knocked back between the seats.

"Give me that ticket," Junior said. "I need it so I can stop the train."

"You're going to stop the train?" C.J. asked.

Henry stopped struggling to get the ticket and looked up at the boy. "Yes," he said, "I've waited for years to find a ticket like that." He grabbed the edge of one seat and pulled himself off Frederick and onto his feet. "I can't stop the train without it."

Frederick stood and helped Laura off the floor.

"That's what we want to do," Sadie said. "We're wasting time fighting if we all want to do the same thing."

"I know you want to stop the train too," Henry said. "Let me do it myself."

"Why?" C.J. asked.

Henry Penny, who seemed to be a powerful man just a few moments earlier, seemed to sag with the weight of his conscience. "This is all my fault," he said. "These people died because of me because I was afraid."

"You were just a boy," C.J. said. "You didn't want to rob the train."

"You're right. I didn't want to rob the train," he said. "If I had, they wouldn't have all died. I need to do this myself."

The man leaned against the seat and stared at the floor with his head bowed.

C.J. looked to Sadie, who nodded her head. He glanced at his other friends, and they all nodded too. Finally, he nodded to Laura.

She went to the man and held the ticket out to him. He raised his head and looked at her. She smiled at him and raised the ticket higher.

The man took the ticket. "Thank you," he said.

He was going to say something more, but then the train started up the hill toward the bridge.

"We're running out of time," Sadie said. "We'll be at the bridge before long."

"You stay here," he told the Young Explorers. "I have to find the conductor."

"We're coming with you," C.J. said.

"There may be trouble," Junior told them.

"We're all in this together," Sadie said, stepping up next to C.J.

"Our lives are on the line too," Frederick said.

"I'm not being left behind," Scotty said, pushing between them and standing in front.

"Let's go," Laura said, peeking out from around them. "Time's wasting."

The tight-knit group of kids gathered together in the aisle showed they had made up their minds.

"Fine," Henry said. "Let's get going then."

He led the group down the aisle toward the blond-haired attendant, who began struggling with the passengers more frantically. Although Henry acted as if he weren't afraid of the attendant, he left as much space as he could between them when he passed by.

"We're trying to help you," Junior told the man.

Each of the Young Explorers squeezed by him without looking at the man.

After that, they headed for the front of the car and the doors through to the next.

When they reached the front of the car, Henry easily pulled it open. He prepared to go through into the next car and stopped.

The train was picking up speed and the wind blowing between the cars buffeted them in the small space. They shivered in the cool night air, made colder by the force of the wind.

"Come on," Henry said, recovering from the blast of wind. He hopped across the space between the cars. "The conductor has to be in this car."

They prepared to follow him one at a time.

Henry opened the door to the next car and stopped. C.J. ran into him and almost lost his balance.

Sadie grabbed C.J.'s arm and kept him from falling to the side and off the train.

"Thanks," C.J. said and then turned his attention back to the man standing in the doorway. He couldn't see past him. When he heard the voice of someone inside the car, he realized why Henry had stopped.

"What's all this then?" a man asked Henry.

C.J. ducked down and looked through the door under Henry's arm. Standing inside the door, the white-haired train attendant prevented them from entering.

"Go back," Henry yelled over his shoulder. The others barely could hear him over the wailing of the wind, but they immediately moved back into the other car.

Once they were all inside the car, Henry turned, jumped across into the car, and pushed the door shut.

"What do we do?" C.J. asked the man.

"Go back," Henry said. "Maybe we can get the drop on him."

"Except that we have the drop on you," the blond attendant said, blocking the way back along the aisle.

The door flew open, revealing the white-haired attendant. "Now we have you," he said.

"Mr. Tallow, I think we have ourselves some stowaways," the blond-haired attendant said.

Mr. Tallow smiled at them with his best fake smile. "I believe you're right, Mr. Wix."

"And do you know what Mr. Tallow and I do with stowaways?" Mr. Wix asked, looking down at Laura with the same fake smile as Mr. Tallow.

Laura hesitated and then said, "You let us go?"

"Oh, no, little lady," Mr. Tallow said. "What we do with stowaways is—"

"—We help them off the train." Mr. Wix laughed.

"Good," C.J. said, "stop the train and let us off."

Mr. Tallow frowned. "I don't think you understand us correctly," he said.

"We help you off the train," Mr. Wix said. "But we don't stop the train first."

"You can't throw all of us off a moving train," Sadie said.

"Certainly we could, Missy," Mr. Tallow told her. "Now come quietly with us and don't make any trouble. There's no need to make things more difficult."

"Yes, no trouble from you," Mr. Wix said. "We don't want to disturb the paying passengers, do we?"

Mr. Tallow opened the door and grabbed Henry's arm while Mr. Wix tried to herd the kids toward it.

Before anyone realized, Henry twisted out of Mr. Tallow's grip and slammed the man against the wall.

"Into the next car," Henry yelled, and without hesitating, the Young Explorers rushed past him and across the gap between the cars.

Once the last of the kids passed, Henry pulled Mr. Tallow away from the wall and shoved him at Mr. Wix, sending both of them to the floor. Before they recovered, he followed the kids into the next car.

They thought they were in the clear, but they had forgotten about the red-haired attendant.

"Whoa there," he told them as they rushed through the door. "There's no running allowed on the train." He glared at the kids and then looked up at Henry. "Are you their father?" he asked.

"No, he's not, Mr. Blaze," Mr. Tallow said, entering the car behind them.

Mr. Wix added, "They're stowaways, Mr. Blaze."

"We don't have time for this," C.J. told them. "We're trying to stop the train."

"Stop the train, you say," Mr. Blaze said. "I don't think that's likely to happen."

"Run," Junior called out, "push by him."

The kids ran forward and tried to swarm by him through the aisle, over the seats or under the seats.

Mr. Tallow and Mr. Wix fell on Henry and tried to drag him to the floor.

Mr. Blaze threw Frederick and Scotty back, knocking Laura to the floor. He caught Sadie by her hair and C.J. by his shirt and was struggling with them when a shot rang out, causing everyone to flinch and stop fighting.

"What is going on?" The conductor asked, his smoking revolver pointed up at the roof of the car.

"These people are stowaways, Sir," Mr. Tallow said. "We were going to put them off the train when they attacked us."

The conductor looked from Mr. Tallow to Mr. Wix. "Is this true?" he asked.

"It's true, Sir," Mr. Wix said.

The conductor tucked the revolver away and adjusted his uniform. "What do you have to say for yourselves?" he asked the others.

"You need to stop the train," Junior said. "The Penny Ante Gang has blocked the bridge."

The conductor frowned at him. "That's ridiculous," he said. "Do any of you have a ticket?"

"I do," Henry said. He pulled the ticket from his pocket and waved it in the air.

The conductor scowled at the kids. "No tickets?"

They all shook their heads.

"Tie them up and put them in the baggage car until we get to our next stop," he told Mr. Blaze. "We'll hand them over to authorities there."

"We're not throwing them off the train?" Mr. Tallow asked. He looked like he was going to cry.

"We don't do that anymore," the conductor told him. "Not on my train, at least."

The three men looked disappointed.

"Stop the train or you'll all die," Henry said, and added, "again."

"If you don't stop trying to make trouble," the conductor said. "We'll tie you up with the others."

"He's telling the truth," C.J. said. "Listen to us."

The conductor looked down at C.J. "I don't have to listen to any of you," he said.

The three attendants grabbed the kids and led them toward the baggage car.

As he passed Henry, C.J. saw the chain of the pocket watch sticking out of Junior's pocket. He twisted out of Mr. Wix's grasp, pulled the watch from Junior's pocket, and ran to the conductor.

The conductor reached for his revolver as Mr. Wix ran to reclaim the boy.

"Do you recognize this, Mr. Olson?" C.J. said, holding the pocket watch out to him. "You dropped it a long time ago."

The conductor looked at the watch, and a faraway look came over his face. As Mr. Wix grabbed the boy, the conductor waved him away.

"I dropped it," he said. "It was a long time ago." He took the watch from C.J.

"It was when the train crashed," C.J. said.

"Crashed?" the man asked as he looked at the watch in his palm.

"Yes," C.J. insisted. "The train crashed off the trestle. You were all killed. Do you remember?"

The conductor clicked it open and looked at the picture for a long moment. He plucked it out and looked at the inscription behind it. "Love, Maggie," he read.

"Do you remember?" C.J. repeated.

"I remember," he said. He looked up at the train attendants. "We have to stop the train."

The train attendants let the kids go as the conductor ran to the front of the car. The rest of them followed him.

Instead of going to the door, he pulled out a keychain and search through the keys. He opened an access panel revealing, among other tools and controls, an emergency signal cord.

The whistle sounded from the engine.

"We're almost at the bridge," the conductor said. He reached into the panel and gave the cord two short pulls to signal to the engineer.

They waited a moment. Nothing happened.

"Didn't it work?" C.J. asked.

The conductor shrugged and reached in again. He pulled the cord twice again and waited.

They felt the train reach the top of the rise and level out. The conductor looked through the window in the door and couldn't see anything in the dark.

"There's no more time," Henry said.

Sadie grabbed C.J.'s hand. "They have to brake," she told him. "They have to."

Tears filled Scotty's eyes. "Are we going to die?" he asked. Laura hugged him and let him cry.

"You're not dead yet," the conductor said and reached back into the panel to pull the cord again.

Suddenly, the car lurched violently, and the force threw them around against the walls.

Frederick and Junior flew backward, out of sight between some seats. The ghostly light that had lit the cars faded and left them in total darkness.

Scotty fell against the wall and hit his head. Laura tumbled against him, and they ended up on the floor in a heap. She tried to push herself up. Her hand slipped in something damp by Scotty's head. She checked Scotty and found that his nose was bleeding. She shook him and called to him. He didn't respond.

C.J. and Sadie also fell to the floor in the dark.

"C.J.," Sadie called, reaching out and trying to find him. "Are you ok?"

"Just bruised," C.J. said, lying close by. "You OK?"

"I'm OK," Sadie said. Her hand found his shoulder. She asked, "We're not going to make it. Are we?"

"I don't know," C.J. said. He took her hand in his. "I don't know."

Chapter 16

The screeching of the locked train wheels as they slid along the track was deafening. C.J. covered his ears with his hands, but that did no good at keeping the high-pitched whine from causing the inside of his head to ache.

He felt it braking. However, they were still moving fast. From the floor, he couldn't tell if they had reached the bridge yet, so he jumped up.

"What are you doing?" Sadie asked. She climbed off the floor and followed as he rushed to a side window of the car.

C.J. climbed across a seat to look out the window. "Are we on the bridge?" he asked.

Sadie looked out over his shoulder. It was dark, and they couldn't see anything.

And then they saw the headlights from a car far below them crossing the lower bridge and heading back toward town. They were on the bridge.

"Are we going to stop in time?" Sadie asked. They were slowing, but C.J. wasn't sure.

C.J. turned until he sat properly and grabbed onto the seat in front of him to brace in case they hit. Sadie dropped into the seat beside him and did the same. They both closed their eyes and waited.

There was a loud bang, followed by several more. The car jolted as it came to an abrupt stop, and then they felt it roll back a little and stop again.

C.J. opened his eyes and looked out the window. "We're still on the bridge," he yelled. "We're still on the bridge, and we've stopped."

Sadie opened her eyes and looked around. "We're alive," she shouted. She grabbed C.J. and hugged him.

He hugged her back. A moment later, they let go of each other and looked for the others.

"We did it," C.J. said. He kicked the floor in front of him and didn't look at Sadie.

Sadie sneaked a peek in C.J.'s direction out of the corner of her eye. "Yes, we did," she said.

They noticed the car was silent. They looked and saw that all the passengers sat silent and unmoving.

"What are they doing?" C.J. whispered.

Sadie shrugged. "I don't know," she said. "I thought it was scary to be on a train full of moving ghosts. This is almost worse."

They heard a moan from the seat behind them. C.J. looked over the back to see Frederick lying on the floor between the seats.

The older boy sat up and rubbed the back of his head. "Did we crash?" he asked.

"No," C.J. said, "the train stopped in time."

Just then, a large hand grabbed the back of the seat across from them, and Henry lumbered up into view. He plopped down on the seat and looked over at the three Young Explorers.

"It stopped," he said. "The train finally stopped." He went to C.J. and held out his hand. "Thank you."

C.J. reached over and shook his hand. "We were happy to help," he said.

Scotty pulled himself up and held a bloody handkerchief over his nose. "We didn't die," Scotty yelled.

Laura and the conductor joined him. "I thought you were dead," Laura said, "all that blood."

"It was just a nosebleed," Scotty said.

"I didn't know that," Laura told him. She turned away from him and crossed her arms.

"You were worried about me," Scotty said, smiling. He was about to punch her in the arm, then stopped when he saw all the unmoving figures seated throughout the car.

The conductor laid his hand on the boy's shoulder and smiled at Henry and all the Young Explorers. "We appreciate what you did for us," he said. "For releasing us from this train and allowing us to move on."

"If I'd just done it when I was a boy," Henry said.

"You came back and stopped it. That counts for something," the conductor told him. He looked at the five Young Explorers. "Now, I believe this is your stop, and the time has come for you to disembark."

They followed the conductor back through the cars. As they moved through the car, the passengers turned and bowed their heads to them in thanks for freeing them.

Mrs. Wesley waited for them at the back of the last coach car. She thanked each one of them.

To C.J., she added, "My granddaughter is on her way here. Please remind her I love her still and give her this." She held out to him the cross-stitch piece she had been working on.

C.J. gingerly took it. "You finished it?" He asked.

"Just in time," Mrs. Wesley said.

C.J. agreed to give it to her granddaughter.

Mrs. Wesley smiled and gave him a hug. Then she returned to her seat to wait.

They made their way to the observation car. It wasn't all the way on the bridge. The conductor opened the door and stepped down. He put down the step, grabbed a lantern, and helped Henry and the Young Explorers off the train.

The conductor put the step away. "We're ready to go," he said. "We are all grateful for your help." He pulled out his gold watch, opened it up and gazed at it for a moment. He snapped it shut and gave it to C.J.

"I can't take it," C.J. said. "It's your wife's picture."

"Keep it as a memento," the conductor told him. "I think she'll be waiting for me at our next stop."

C.J. put the watch in his pocket along with the cross-stitch. The six of them backed away from the train as the conductor mounted the steps.

"All aboard." The conductor waved his lantern.

They heard shouts from the woods down the hill. People called their names. Frederick called back. "We're here," he yelled, "by the old trestle bridge."

"Good bye," Henry said to the kids. "You had better hurry home."

"Aren't you coming with?" Sadie asked.

"No," Henry said. "I reckon it's time for me to move on."

C.J. shook his hand. "You did good," he told the man. "One hundred souls can now rest."

Henry smiled at C.J., and they all wished him well.

The five walked to the edge of the bluff and looked down at the lights in the town below. The woods along the track leading down the hill were dark except for an occasional flash of a lantern.

Then, several people broke free of the trees next to the track and spotted them standing at the top of the hill. Their fathers called to them and ran up the hill toward them.

Laura and Scotty ran down to the adults. Before long they were in the arms of their parents and talking a mile a minute, telling them the story of their adventures on the Phantom Express.

Frederick walked down too. Sadie followed and then turned to C.J. "Come on," she said, "Let's go."

"Go on ahead," C.J. said. "I'll be there in a minute."

Sadie nodded and followed Frederick until their parents enveloped them in hugs and gave their versions of the Phantom Express story.

The train whistle blew, and C.J. turned to see that the conductor had closed up the car. The engine rolled forward and with a bang and a lurch, each car moved.

C.J. waved to the train. He didn't know whether anyone looked out at him, but he waved all the same.

Then he noticed Henry was gone.

He turned back to the slope and saw that his dad hurried up toward him.

"Are you all right?" Angus asked. "Are you hurt?"

C.J. shook his head. "I'm fine. We're all fine."

"What happened to all of you?" Angus asked. "How did you get on the train?"

C.J. took a breath. The excitement on the train finally caught up to him. "I'm kind of tired, Dad. Can I tell you later?" he asked.

Angus nodded and gave him a hug. "I love you."

"I love you too, Dad," C.J. said.

C.J. realized that the sound of the train had faded away. He turned and looked at the bridge. The train was gone, and the bridge was empty.

"Have any of you seen Mr. Penny?" Angus asked. "It's like he disappeared."

C.J. smiled and turned back to his father. "He finished what he needed to do," the boy said. "He won't be back here again."

Their reunion with their parents and the stories about what happened on the train went on for more than an hour. As the kids' excitement changed to exhaustion, they started back down the hill.

They found the cars parked along the side of the road. After loading everyone up, they turned around and headed back toward town.

C.J. pulled the watch out of his pocket and opened it. He looked at the picture of the conductor's wife a moment and then asked, "Do you think the conductor will find his wife where they are going?"

Angus glanced over at his son and the watch and thought for a moment. "Yes," he said, finally. "Yes, I think he will."

When they pulled up to the train station, they found a small crowd gathered there. The sheriff talked with his deputies while the mayor and curator waited nearby.

The sheriff held up his hand for the deputies to wait where they were and hurried over to the cars. The mayor and curator rushed up right behind him.

"Did you find them all?" the sheriff asked.

"All five of the kids are here, safe and sound," Angus told him.

"Except for my nose," Scotty said.

"Except for that," Angus agreed.

"Where did you find them?" the sheriff asked. "I had people looking everywhere."

"They were at the top of the bluff by the trestle," Angus told him. "Somehow they'd gotten on the train while it was here at the station."

The sheriff looked past Angus at C.J. "You were on the train?" the sheriff asked.

C.J. nodded. "We stopped it," he said. "The Phantom Express won't be coming back."

"Thank God for that," the mayor said. The curator nodded in agreement.

"Actually," Angus told him, "you have our Young Explorers here to thank for that." He reached over and rumpled C.J.'s hair.

"What about Henry Penn?" the sheriff asked, and then he corrected himself. "Henry Penny, I mean."

"Henry Penny is gone for good," Angus told them. "I don't think you have any worries about him."

"No worries at all," a man said. "Though I'm not gone for good." Henry Penny walked into the middle of the group, holding his hands up. "I've come to surrender to you, Sheriff."

Startled by his sudden appearance, it took a moment before the sheriff or his deputies responded. The sheriff ordered one of his deputies to put handcuffs on the man.

"I thought you'd be long gone," C.J. said.

"I ran away once," Henry said, "but not again."

"What about the debate?" the curator asked the mayor. "Your opponent will be in jail."

"You no longer have an opponent," C.J. said. "I guess that means you're going to win the election."

"We may have to postpone the election," the sheriff said, "until after the trial. In case someone still wants to run against him."

Everyone laughed, except for the mayor.

"We'll see," the mayor said. "We'll see."

"The ticket is gone," C.J. told the curator. "Laura used it to get on the train. The conductor kept it."

"Oh well," the curator said. "I'm sure there are other treasures waiting for us out in the river."

"I'm sure there is," Angus told him. "Right now, I think it's time for these kids to get some rest."

After agreeing to meet with them again in the morning, Angus wished them a good night and turned the car around and headed back to the house.

When they pulled up in front of the Prairie Rose, they found another car parked there already with a woman who was pulling luggage out of the trunk.

While everyone else filed up the walk to the porch, Angus stopped to help the woman.

"Are you Miss Wesley?" Angus asked her.

"Yes, I am," the woman said. "I'm Clara Wesley. Are you Mr. Kask?"

Angus nodded. "Can we help you with your luggage?" he asked.

She sighed. "That would be wonderful," she said.

Angus and C.J. took her bags and walked with her up to the house.

"Are you Mrs. Wesley's granddaughter?" C.J. asked, lugging one large suitcase up the steps.

Clara looked back at the boy. "Yes," she said. "Ruth Wesley was my grandmother. She and my grandfather built this house."

C.J. and Angus dropped the luggage at the bottom of the stairs in the entryway.

"It's a beautiful old house," C.J. said. "I've enjoyed staying here."

"Thank you," Clara said. "I love it too."

"Unfortunately, you missed your grandmother," Angus said. "She had her bags packed this morning. I'm not sure where she went or how long she would be gone, but she left sometime today."

The woman looked at Angus in confusion. "I don't know what you mean."

"Your grandmother," Angus said. "The woman living in this house. She left earlier today."

"I'm not sure who you're referring to," Clara said, frowning. "My grandmother died thirty years ago."

"Thirty years ago?" Angus asked.

"She was on the Express that crashed off the bridge," Clara told him. "She was on her way to visit me and my parents in Oregon."

"Then who was that woman who was living here?" Angus asked. "She said she was Mrs. Ruth Wesley."

"She was," C.J. said, "we saw her on the train."

"The train?" Clara asked.

Angus told her about the Phantom Express and how the kids had stopped it from crashing yet again.

Clara looked as if she might faint. Angus helped her to the rocking chair in the front parlor. Everyone else gathered in the room as well.

"There is something else," C.J. said. "As we got off the train, your grandmother gave me this for you." He pulled out the cross-stitch and handed it to her.

It had a pink rose with the words "For my granddaughter, Clara, with love forever." In the bottom corner, she had stitched the words "Grandma Ruth" with the dates "1805-1883" in fancy letters.

Clara's eyes immediately filled with tears, and Edna hurried over to her with a handkerchief.

"It's been a long day," Edna said. "I think it's time that we all get some rest." She asked the men to take the woman's luggage up to her bedroom; the same one that old Mrs. Wesley had said was hers.

After everyone had gone to bed, the five Young Explorers, unable to sleep after the night's excitement, gathered in C.J.'s room once again to talk about what had happened on the train.

While the others talked excitedly about battling train attendants and ghosts, C.J. went to the window and looked out at the trestle bridge barely visible in the dim moonlight. He pulled out the gold pocket watch and held it up to reflect the light from the lamp in the room.

"Do you believe in fate?" Sadie asked as she joined him at the window.

"Fate?" C.J. asked.

"Mrs. Wesley said that dying in the train crash was their fate," Sadie said.

"I don't know," C.J. said, gazing out at the night sky again. "But if it exists, I wonder what fate has in store for us next."

Don't miss out!

Visit the website below and you can sign up to receive emails whenever S T Cameron publishes a new book. There's no charge and no obligation.

https://books2read.com/r/B-A-CWRB-BSBRG

BOOKS 2 READ

Connecting independent readers to independent writers.

Also by S T Cameron

The Young Explorers
Inca Wraith
Phantom Express
Scottish Knight

Watch for more at www.stcameron.com.

About the Author

I tell stories and have adventures.When I was a little boy, I would tell stories and have adventures in the backyard pretending I was in a circus in front of an audience of my family and neighbors. In elementary school, more stories and adventures were played out on the stage in front of my class and, sometimes, the entire school.In High School and College, I donned my glasses and disguised my super writer self in my computer nerd persona and while I still told stories and had adventures, they were never made publicly known.Many years later, I decided that it was time to remove my disguise and let my stories out in the world again.Outside of writing, I have adventures with Kay, my wife and future author of her own books, my two wonderful daughters and their families including four grand-children and two grand-puppies. I also let people know what is going on with my writing at stcameron.com.

Read more at www.stcameron.com.

www.ingramcontent.com/pod-product-compliance
Lightning Source LLC
Chambersburg PA
CBHW020624250626
47154CB00004B/1661